DESERVING OF MURDER

MARY ANN NOE

Black Rose Writing | Texas

The author grants the final approval for this literary material.

First printing

This is a work of fiction. Names, characters, businesses, places, events, and incidents are either the products of the author's imagination or used in a fictitious manner. Any resemblance to actual persons, living or dead, or actual events is purely coincidental.

ISBN: 978-1-68513-498-3
PUBLISHED BY BLACK ROSE WRITING
www.blackrosewriting.com

Printed in the United States of America
Suggested Retail Price (SRP) $18.95

Deserving of Murder is printed in Gentium Book Basic

*As a planet-friendly publisher, Black Rose Writing does its best to eliminate unnecessary waste to reduce paper usage and energy costs, while never compromising the reading experience. As a result, the final word count vs. page count may not meet common expectations.

For Pam, who will admit, if you ask her,
that she can get lost on a staircase.

and

For all the workers at Ten Chimneys.

DESERVING OF MURDER

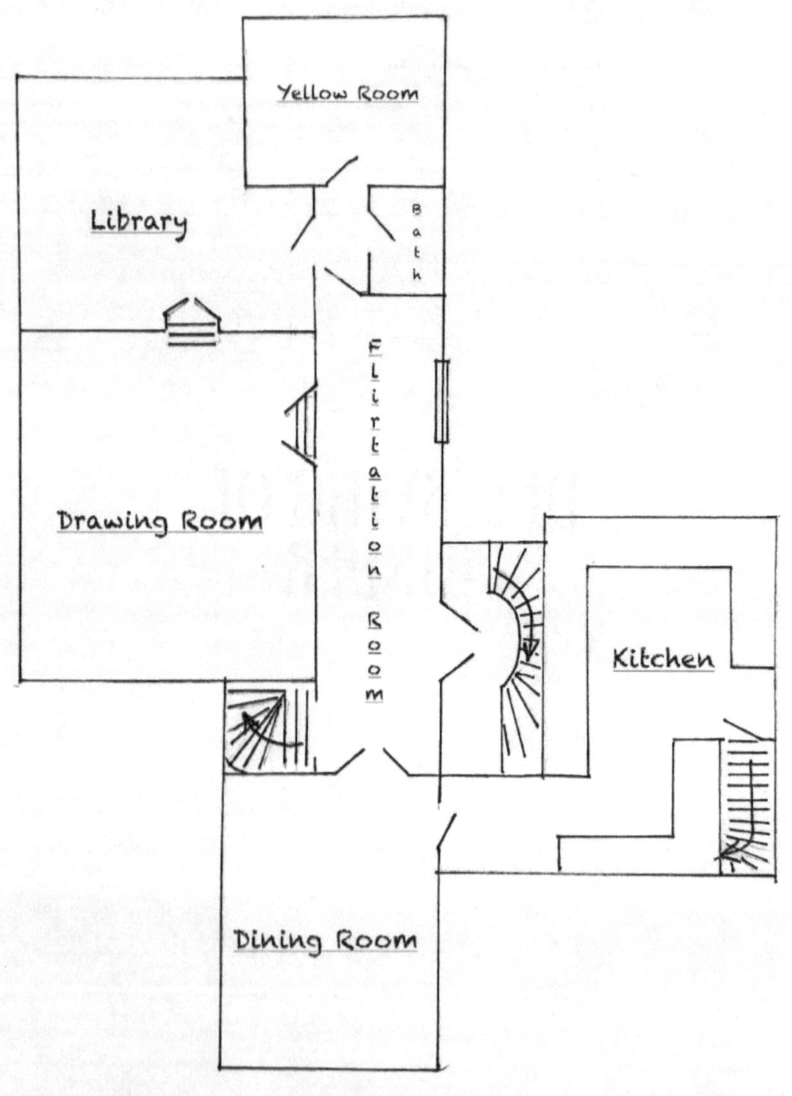

Lynn and Alfred's Country House

-1-

Nobody was outside, and the snow was still falling, piling up in corners, collecting in deep drifts. The white scarf didn't even show against the snowbanks.

On the estate, the chicken coop and the pig barn were silent, the animals were gone, serving the purpose they were raised for, butchered and wrapped, some packages in the freezer, some given as gifts.

The two cows, munching calmly in their stalls in the barn, were cozy in their shared body heat. The thick walls shut out the weather, stymying the snow that tried to seep into any cracks. But it found none. The studio was shut up for the winter, another building too tight for the howling wind. Still, the snow created barricades against both.

The edges of the greenhouse, the creamery, and even the poolhouse were softened by the drifts embracing their walls. The only buildings that seemed even a bit immune to the onslaughts of the storm were the red cottage on the rise above the pool and the main house tucked into the dip down below. Both had height and substance enough to turn their shoulders to the storm and ride it out.

The outside light on the cottage porch glowed, but only showed when the wind stopped to take a breath. Other than that, the windows of the cottage were dark, the guests bundled somewhere inside. If they had any intelligence at all, they would be wrapped in heavy blankets pulled up to their noses.

Inside the main house, those who were still up—and there were a few—were mostly in the drawing room, draped on various pieces of furniture, finishing up brandies or whiskeys or whatevers, and soaking up the heat from the fireplace.

Outside, the entire estate was quiet, blanketed against the cold by snow, deep and luscious, like rich vanilla ice cream. No one was outside in that wicked weather. No one, unless you counted the body wearing the scarf.

The scarf didn't show against the white, except for the blood. If not for the darkness, the spray of blood surely would have.

-2-

New York City lifted its shoulders and turned its back to the wind, but it didn't improve things. The weather turned bitter cold on top of the wind and unending gloom, which made the huffing and chuffing from the huge diesel Pullman train waiting at the platform even more dramatic. Destined for Chicago, the exquisite blue and silver Art Deco 20th Century Limited was poised in New York's Grand Central Station, primed for receiving its usual plethora of well-heeled passengers heading west.

The platform was a bustle of activity, though that was tapering off now, as most passengers were already aboard, the women with their complimentary high-fashion perfumes, the men with carnations. Red Caps lifted the last of the luggage from the trolleys into the cars, some to be stored and retrieved later, some to go to the sleeping compartments of the guests. Already, several passengers were seated at the windows of the observation car, drinks in hand, anticipating the lovely views to come along the Hudson River. Though the sun set early this time of year, there would be a moon to provide a bit of light.

Lynn stood on the train platform, gathering her wits about her as a Red Cap lifted her luggage from the trolley and handed it off to the Pullman porter waiting at the steps of the train.

"There you are, Miss Fontanne," the Red Cap said. "The rest of your luggage is in the baggage car."

"Thank you, sir," Lynn said, handing off a hefty tip. She was one of the few women who didn't answer to the appellation Mrs. So-and-So. She was always Miss Fontanne, not Mrs. Alfred Lunt. Yes, they were known together as The Lunts, but if someone called out to "Mrs. Lunt," she never twitched.

Lynn waited, albeit not very patiently, below the steps to their assigned sleeping car. She rolled Pullman's miniature perfume bottle from one gloved hand to the other. Realizing that what she was doing showed too much nervousness, she slipped the little bottle into her coat pocket, and sighed. Another mannerism to tuck away to use on stage, but not here in public.

She wasn't terribly worried about Alfred, who was never late, though this was getting close. She and Alfred always took the drawing room suite, which gave them ample room for Alfred's 6-foot-plus frame. This trip, they reserved a second sleeper, though smaller, for the couple travelling with them. That is, if the others ever appeared. Ed Wright's wife, Harriet, assured them, just this morning, in fact, they would both be there. Lynn wondered if Ed was having one of his fits of pique. They needed his writing skills to polish the play. Ten Chimneys, their estate out in Wisconsin, might be the only place to hold him in line.

Lynn opened her purse and got out her compact mirror. She tucked in a loose strand of dark hair under her mink toque. Along with the compact, she tucked the thought of the others being late into her purse, and clicked the latch shut. Lynn, a fashion maven if there ever was one, was instantly recognizable as Broadway's premier actress, along with her actor husband, Alfred. Because of her impeccable posture, she looked taller than she was as she wrapped her mink coat tighter to keep out the cold. Indoors, her complexion was flawless, creamy even with only moisturizer. But here, on the platform, roses bloomed on her cheeks and the perfect bow of her lipstick couldn't hide the slight tremble from the cold. Even with her shoulders hunched under the mink, she was lovely. Never considered truly gorgeous, nonetheless, she knew how to carry herself, dress well, and use gestures and movements to advantage. Standing on the red carpet that stretched from engine to the ticket takers at the entrance to the platform, she was grateful that others granted her the privacy to tap her foot in the only move that showed her concern. But by now, the platform was almost empty of all but the railroad employees.

"Finally!" she breathed as she saw the tall man in a belted overcoat and fashionable brown tweed fedora heading her way along the carpet.

Alfred Lunt. Her other half. He was considerably taller than Lynn, and carried a solid frame speaking of equally solid good work. His face, the summer gardening tan lost, held an open, welcoming look. Besides radiating interest in others, his best feature were his warm brown eyes, always alert, curious, contemplative at times. Every woman on earth fell in love with him.

She sent him a smile as he advanced.

The Red Cap bustled up with the last of their cases and handed them off to the Pullman porter with a bob of the head. Alfred rushed in behind him and offered a generous tip, along with the instructions to load certain bags into their compartment and hand off the others to be stored until Chicago. Hopefully, the latter would show up when they themselves did. They had plenty of experience with props, costumes and luggage going AWOL between New York City and some far-flung town where they were scheduled to perform. Lynn and Alfred exchanged glances that said it all: *We can only hope.*

The Red Cap, enlisting help from a compatriot, scurried off to carry out Alfred's instructions. The Pullman porter handed Alfred the customary carnation, which he secured in his coat's lapel buttonhole with a "Thanks, George." The porter stepped up into the train, leaving the couple waiting on the platform. Waiting and fretting.

"Where *are* they?" Lynn shaded her eyes to peer down the platform. "They should be here by now. It's almost six. The train won't wait."

"They'll be here." Alfred's voice, usually so soothing to Lynn, betrayed a bit of doubt.

She caught it. "Do you think this was a bad idea, Alfred? Ed is known to be rather…"

"Difficult?" Alfred said.

"Just so," Lynn replied. "We chased him all over town. He never answered our phone calls. You even sent him a telegram. All we ever got was an 'I'll get back to you soon.'"

"But it was your brilliant idea to go through his wife." Alfred put his arm across her shoulders and pulled her close. He kissed the top of her head. "You're shivering! Did you dress for the weather? Besides your fur coat, I mean." He sent her an indulgent smile.

Lynn hunched her shoulders, bringing her collar closer to her neck. Under the fur coat, she wore a wool skirt and sweater, which should have kept her warm as well as chic. She looked up at her husband. Dark eyes sparkled below brows fashioned by her expert hand. "Of course I dressed appropriately, Alfred. You're just trying to distract me." She hated to admit that she was still cold.

She glanced down the platform again. No sign of Ed and Harriet. She stirred in Alfred's embrace.

Not only was she physically cold, she was heart-cold. She turned to look outside, past the train. The outdoors that she could glimpse at the far end of the platform was dismal and dark, even though it was not yet night. The winter clouds were so low, they were in danger of being scraped raw by the buildings. The snow lay sulking on the ground, as if resentful of the additional piles of dirty snow plowed up from the streets. A film of grit covered everything, snow, street, buildings. The only reason the trees escaped the onslaught was their constant shuddering and shaking in the wind.

Alfred kept his arm across her shoulders, swiveling with her. She lifted her hand to grasp his. "Oh, Alfred, I am so tired of this…this…"

She waved her free hand at the sight outside. "I usually love New York, but this…"

"I agree," Alfred said. "I thought this would be such a wonderful interlude in our touring. We could enjoy the city before we headed out on the road again." He shook his head. "It was not to be. Not with this weather."

"Not with the stagehands strike either," Lynn said. "We can't even rehearse, much less play."

"I'm sorry, Lynnie."

"It's not your fault, Alfred." She gave her husband's hand a squeeze. "But I so looked forward to the exhilaration of the Broadway stage again. We've played on the road for the past how many months? I was ready to come home to our own bed after a performance. But there's no performance to come home after."

"I know. I'm disappointed too. It's such a letdown," Alfred said.

"It feels like I've stepped off a ten-foot ledge into quicksand, and I'm sinking." She leaned into Alfred and set her head on his shoulder. To plant a kiss on his cheek, Lynn was obliged to stretch a bit. She patted his hand. "What are we going to do with ourselves now that we can't mount a show? You must be going crazy."

"I *am* going crazy," Alfred admitted, then shifted gears. "From all I've heard, money talks with Ed, and we're paying him well. So, this should work out just fine."

"Well," Lynn said, "If he's the *bon vivant* everyone says he is, Wisconsin may not exactly be his cup of tea."

"His wife said he thought he'd be going out to barbarian territory," Alfred said.

"Barbarian territory!" Lynn smiled. "He's a New Yorker who hasn't looked any farther west than Buffalo, and perhaps not even that far. At least he agreed to come."

"It doesn't really matter, does it," Alfred said. "Once we get out to Ten Chimneys, where is he going to go? What is he going to do out there but work? It's pretty isolated, especially in the winter."

Lynn said, "You did call Ben to turn up the heat in the main house as well as the cottage?"

Alfred nodded. "Yes, the heat's up, the water's on. But they won't be able to cook up in the cottage. Ben said the stove is on the fritz."

"We'll bring them down to the main house for meals. I hope they won't mind tromping through the snow to get there."

"We just won't tell them about that until we're there. It's not that far from cottage to house anyway." They shared a low chuckle.

"Did you tell them about the train, and how wonderful it is?" Lynn asked.

"I thought I'd hold that in reserve, just in case my charm couldn't convince them."

That drew a sparkling smile from Lynn. "Who can refuse you, darling?"

"I'm just glad we could talk them into it. We'll put him to work and actually accomplish something."

"From your mouth to God's ear."

-3-

Lynn moved a little away from Alfred and looked back down the platform to where the ticket taker, pointing their way, seemed to be rushing two passengers along the length of the red carpet toward them.

Alfred turned to follow her gaze. "Look, isn't that them just coming along now?" He took a step forward. "Yes, that's Ed and Harriet."

Lynn puffed out a breath of relief as the two jogged close enough to be recognized, followed by a Red Cap with their bags on a trolley. "Come on, you two! Let's go!"

The Pullman porter came over and handed Harriet a bottle of perfume, but Ed waved off the boutonniere offered.

The conductor stepped down from the train and hollered, "All aboard!"

The four hustled to climb aboard before the porter could pull up the step and slide the door shut. Even before they reached their sleeping compartments, the train gave a raucous whistle and soft bump as it eased out of the station.

"Milwaukee, here we come," Ed Wright said, as the porter of their carriage hoisted their bags into place, and disappeared down the corridor.

"When you've settled in, come on into our drawing room, and we'll brief you about this little junket," Alfred said.

The Lunts' suite was ample and comfortable, with a full sofa and a pair of red leather lounge chairs, in addition to two full-size beds and a private bathroom. No matter how often they traveled on the Century, Lynn always marveled at the sumptuous appointments. Walnut paneling with brass trim, pristine linens and plush towels. A lounge car and club cars with drinks made to order, served by the officious staff. A couple of dining cars with food to die for.

Ed and Harriet Wright appeared at the Lunts' door before the train was fully out of the station. Ed still had his coat on, because "these trains are always cold." Harriet appeared to agree with him, considering her coat remained on too. The four of them looked out the window at the receding cityscape as they picked up speed.

"How long before we get to Milwaukee?" Harriet asked, taking off her hat and setting it on a tiny table. Released, her amber hair spilled down, some obscuring one of her lovely green eyes. She was a tall woman, taller than her husband, but she didn't appear to lord it over him. She stood, unbuckled and unbuttoned her long grey-blue wool suit coat and hung it on a nearby hook, then dropped into one of the red leather chairs by the large window. She leaned back into the shadows, where her scars were less obvious. *Horrible car accident,* Lynn remembered.

"Chicago first," Alfred said. "Then we change for Milwaukee."

Lynn took up the litany. "Then a change to Genesee Depot."

Ed groaned. He seemed to have a permanent–what was it? Not a scowl, exactly. More like the potential of a scowl. "So, we're on this train forever. Is that what you're saying?"

"No, darling," Lynn said. She'd been warned of his sometimes prickly personality. Success bred a sense of entitlement in some people, it seemed. "We have about sixteen hours to enjoy the ride to Chicago, then a couple of hours or so before we reach Milwaukee to change trains again. About an hour later, we get into Genesee Depot. But I find that the gentle sway of a train is a lovely soporific for sleeping the night away."

That drew only a "Humph" from Ed. He unwound his scarf and shrugged out of his camel hair coat. After stuffing the scarf into a pocket, he flung the coat over one of the chairs. He took off his hat and added it to the pile.

Lynn smiled. *Too cold? Clearly not. Not on the Century where everything was attuned to travelers' comforts.*

"This will be fun, darling," Harriet said, giving his arm a squeeze. She stood and picked up his coat and hat, adding them to a hook next to hers, before returning to her seat.

Ed seemed to melt a bit. "With you, my dear, life is always fun."

Well! Lynn thought. *Apparently, he's not a total ogre. At least with Harriet.* "You'll be refreshed after a good night's sleep, Ed. Guaranteed."

"But you don't have to sleep the night away, Ed," Alfred said. "We need dinner first."

"Dinner." Ed sounded as if he didn't believe it.

"Of course, dear," Lynn said. "You haven't had time to check the menu, have you? It's right there next to the door. Take a peek."

"Chipped beef on toast? Wilted lettuce? Cold coffee?" Ed didn't look at the menu.

Alfred laughed. He swiveled to peer at the menu on the wall. "Well, let's see. Tonight's meal begins with caviar, followed by a number of entrée choices: filet mignon, lobster, stuffed eggs and ham, salmon, prime rib. Shall I go on? That's just a taste of what is offered."

"I hope the food is hot." Ed again.

"Oh, darling, according to Lynn and Alfred, everything about this train is top-notch. If the food is up to their standards, I'm sure it's absolutely marvelous."

"All served on specially commissioned Pullman china and crystal. Linen napkins and tablecloths, and flowers at every table. We could be dining at the best in the city, from the tastes and looks of it all. And impeccable service to boot," Lynn said.

Harriet said, "Sounds divine."

"So, let's go!" Alfred said. "We'll be out of the city shortly, and we can claim a nice table in one of the dining cars."

"Darling," Lynn said, "there are no tables that are not nice. Lovely big windows. Although, I'll concede it's dark enough that the scenery won't be especially stellar. If we go down to dine now, we can take our time. They never make people feel they have to eat and rush out. All very leisurely."

"Grand," Harriet said. "I'm ready."

Ed strode to the door and opened it. "Are you coming, or not?" He stepped out into the corridor.

Lynn's look sent to Alfred said, *Give it a minute. He doesn't know where he's going.*

Ed's voice came back to them. "Where's the dining car?"

"Just two cars away, sir, that direction. Watch your step at the coupling." The deep voice of their car's conductor.

"Come on, would ya?" Ed's voice. "Now I'm hungry."

By the time they made their way to the dining car, Ed secured a table halfway down, tucked behind one of the Art Deco dividers. "Over here!" he called.

"Oh, Ed!" Harriet whispered. "Must you be a bull in a china shop?" She hurried ahead to join her husband, and apparently shush him into his seat.

Lynn and Alfred followed behind, nodding occasionally to people seated at tables along the way. People respected their privacy, for the most part, though there were sometimes fans awed by their presence. However, not on the Century. Discretion on the part of the servers and the other employees ensured a relaxing trip.

Harriet subdued Ed enough so that he was only tapping his knife on the tabletop, rather than spouting his impatience with words. Alfred held the chair for Lynn, who slid in with practiced grace.

The waiter approached, bent to them, and asked for drink orders. Turning to Lynn, he cocked his head and said, "Madam? A cocktail for you and your friend?" He indicated Harriet.

"She'll have a dry martini," Ed said.

But Harriet frowned at him, then turned to Lynn. "What are you having?"

"I favor champagne and dry white wine." Lynn answered. She looked up at the waiter. "One, please."

"Make it two," Harriet said, without looking at Ed.

"Fine," Ed said, a scowl evident in his voice. "I'll take the dry martini then."

"And you, sir?" The waiter set his attention on Alfred.

"A Manhattan, please," Alfred said. "That always wakes up my appetite."

Lynn could see the waiter scanning his domain, but never hovering over anyone that did not beckon him. Once the drinks were delivered, Alfred called for the menu. It took little time, in spite of the extensive selections, for anyone to make a choice. The waiter materialized just as Alfred turned to call him over.

"Sir, what would you like this evening?" No notepad spoiled the formality of the waiter's uniform.

"Are you going to remember everything?" Ed's voice showed up the skeptic.

"Of course, sir." The waiter smiled and clasped his hands behind his back.

"All right, then. Let's see what you can do with this." Ed rattled off, "Crab Louis cocktail, veal cutlet, bread, apple pie."

"Very good, sir." The waiter turned to the women. "And for you, ladies?" He never twitched at the affrontery of Ed ordering first.

Lynn and Harriet opted for iced tomato juice and Russian caviar to start, followed by planked salmon steaks. Harriet ordered the apple pie, but Lynn veered to the caramel custard. Alfred opened with hot clam bouillon–"something I don't make at home," he confessed–followed by the hearty roast prime rib with vegetables and potatoes.

"So, what do you expect from me?" Ed asked. "The first act moves along fine, but, by the middle of the second act, it–"

Harriet held up her hand. "Nope. No business talk during dinner. Them's the rules, kiddo."

Lynn expected Ed to come out with some searing remark. It was a pleasant surprise to hear nothing from him. He held out his hands in a gesture of surrender, but didn't say a word. He picked up his martini and settled back in his seat.

Dinner proceeded at a leisurely pace, with mere small talk about the weather, of course, the Broadway season, and the stagehands' strike.

After dessert and coffee, Alfred pushed back his chair and declared himself sated.

"Well, darling," Lynn said, "you certainly did yourself proud with that prime rib. I must admit, the salmon was divine. But I think we should head back. There are people coming in for a late dinner. Let's make room for them."

The four arose and made their way back to Lynn and Alfred's suite, where Harriet chose a chair near a window and Lynn slipped one foot out of her shoe and tucked it under her as she sat down on the sofa.

"Say, how about we relax for a bit, and then," Alfred said, "a drink to close out the evening?"

"There's a bar?" Harriet said.

Alfred nodded. "A bar, a club car, an observation car–"

"What's to observe? Snow, snow and more snow." Ed's tone sounded rather childish.

"You are so lucky to be on the Century," Lynn said, in an attempt to mollify. "If we took the Pennsylvania, we'd be looping up and down over mountains, which certainly wouldn't make for a wholesome journey."

Alfred picked up the accolades for the Century. "This train follows the Hudson River, then along the Great Lakes, so the road is smooth and level. Perfect for a good night's sleep before we get into Chicago."

"Right." Ed's tone was hardly different. "It's winter. It gets dark early. Still not much to look at then, in the dark."

Lynn shared a look of *I'd sigh if it weren't so impolite* with Alfred.

"Ed," Alfred said, "let's go up to the club car. The girls can come along–"

"Not me," Harriet said. "I'm pooped. This chair is too comfortable to pry myself out of." She waved her hand at the men, who were already standing. "Go, go. Have fun."

"I'll stay here with Harriet," Lynn said. "But would you order a nice highball for me and have it sent down, please?" She turned to Harriet. "Something for you, Harriet?"

Harriet waved a no-thanks, then turned back to the window. Her head began to nod gently in time to the tracks' click-clack almost as soon as the men slid the door to the compartment shut.

Lynn turned her attention to anticipating the return to their beloved Wisconsin estate. She would leave conversation for another time.

A bustling Broadway career was undeniably wonderful, but for peace, one couldn't beat the estate nestled near a small town in Wisconsin. During the summer, the estate was the definition of pleasure, a true getaway from the zigs and zags of New York City. There was a barn and a corn crib, a greenhouse and a chicken coop. With chickens. There were cows and horses, pigs and a pet goose. There was a pool, and a poolhouse with a shower. There was a guesthouse, converted from an old chicken coop into a cottage, painted red for a splash of color.

And gardens. Flowers everywhere: delphiniums, marigolds, cleomes, bleeding heart, hydrangeas and hostas, gladioli. An orchard of multiple trees, some of which were undoubtedly surprised to find themselves in a northern climate, lay behind an extensive vegetable garden with corn, beans, squash, peas, tomatoes—oodles of tomatoes—all waiting to be put up in the fall, or set out on a produce stand at the end of the driveway.

But the gem of it all was the main house. Perched on the edge of a deep dip, the white siding and green shutters were a welcome refuge from the brick and mortar of New York.

All of this, the entire estate, was situated on ground that undulated, as if languorous subterranean pythons held a convention decades ago. It made for ridges, and pots the size of ponds, and soft rolling lawns between the buildings.

Years before, when Lynn stepped out at the village depot for the first time, all doubts of being out in the boonies were erased. The little town was charming, with a couple of taverns, a church, a post office, a huddled handful of houses, and not too much more. When Lynn left New York, she wondered what she was getting into. First, change trains in Chicago, then again in Milwaukee, then... Smaller and smaller trains, cities to small towns, to, finally, that village, where Alfred, the man she loved, met her at the depot.

Lynn knew he was the man for her when, at first meeting in New York, he came offstage and fell down a short flight of stairs, landing at her feet. He looked up at her and said, in that wonderful voice of his, "Hello, love." The rest, as the saying goes, was history. So, she married him.

The estate became her retreat, just as it was for him. They worked like Furies in the city throughout the theater season, then decamped for the country each summer. Of course, they didn't leave theater behind them. They took it with them, dragging initially reluctant directors, actors, friends, writers, out to the estate, so they could work without the vagaries of city interruptions. One trip was all it took, and everyone clamored for an invitation.

Which is why they were at the estate in the middle of winter. To get out of the city and work. The stagehands were on strike, unusual in the middle of a season, but there you were, it happened. Their dear friend, Noël Coward, persuaded Lynn and Alfred to gather the people most important to their next play, and remove to the estate. They could get ever so much work done.

And so, in spite of an impending winter storm predicted to sweep out of the plains states and into Wisconsin, they nabbed Ed Wright, the playwright, sweetened the deal by inviting his wife, Harriet, and boarded the train. The other four invited would follow on a later train.

With a soft knock at the door, Lynn's highball appeared. Once she had it in hand, she went to the small sofa, cuddled herself into a corner and lifted her legs to stretch out. A small sip, and she felt herself relaxing.

-4-

Lynn was jolted back to the reality of the gentle swaying of the train, and the insistent clicking of the wheels on the rails, by a sudden snort from Harriet's direction. She peered at Harriet to see her scrubbing her face with her hands. Lynn scooched up a bit and curled into the corner of the couch.

Harriet dropped her hands to her lap and opened her eyes, only to come in contact with Lynn's gaze. "Oh my dear! Was I snoring? Did I startle you? I certainly startled myself." She liberated a chuckle.

Lynn smiled and reached for her drink. "Not to worry. I wasn't sleeping. Only lost in a reverie of the Wisconsin estate in the summer. I wish you could see it then." She was rambling a bit to give Harriet time to pull herself back into the here and now. "The woods are gorgeous, what with the oaks and such. Maybe tomorrow will be clear enough to see some of the scenery on the way to Genesee Depot." She took a sip of her highball.

"If I can stay awake long enough to enjoy it!" Harriet said, swiveling her chair so she faced Lynn. "We've been working nonstop, so it'll be wonderful to be able to set a slower pace. No New York phone ringing off the hook. No producers calling to get final pages. And on and on."

No need to run interference because of Ed either. Lynn thought it best not to say it. "You must be exhausted. This will give you a bit of a break anyway, we hope."

Harriet nodded. She sat up straight, sending her arms stretching overhead and spreading her fingers into starfish. "I love Ed dearly, but sometimes..." She smiled, in spite of the implications the silent moment offered.

"Ed clearly adores you," Lynn said. "How did you two meet? I hope I'm not being too forward." She was truly interested how these two disparate people managed to...collide?

Harriet's laugh was deep and long. "It's quite a story, believe me. Would you like the short version or the long version?"

Lynn joined her laughter to Harriet's. "It seems we have plenty of time, now that we're both awake. Feed me the long version, please." As a second thought, she added, "Would you like something to drink?"

Harriet shook her head. "It would just make me tired, even if it's coffee. Strange how my body reacts that way." She slid her feet out of her shoes and curled up in the chair. "The long version. Right." She cleared her throat. "Here goes."

•   •   •

Harriet's life was a long strand of fortunate events. An idyllic California childhood, followed by a successful and adored high school career. College was a breeze, earning her a journalism degree, with a splash of drama on the side. With her auburn hair and green eyes, she was a knockout. Most boys backed off a bit when they saw how tall she was, usually a head more than they were. She didn't mind. Harriet was focused on becoming a Career Woman.

Even before graduation, she snagged the plum of a job writing a gossip column for a regional newspaper favored by the middle-class Hollywood crowd. It wasn't the *Los Angeles Times*, but it was a good solid job. She wrote under the pseudonym Tilly Williams, which allowed her to do restaurant critiques as well, without being recognized. Incorporated within her column, she handed out advice under the heading, Tell Tilly. She unearthed some gossipy gems, but nothing on the level of her fellow columnists at the bigger LA papers. Her editor preserved her anonymity, and she could write at home and courier her work to the paper. Perfect.

She hobnobbed as Harriet Stevens, her real name, with upcoming actors and others in the industry, attending parties, concerts, dances, anywhere she could pick up tidbits. All without anyone knowing she was Tilly. Tilly went on to be known as Tell-All Tilly, a nickname Harriet found hilarious.

At first, Harriet was afraid the stars and upper crust she was writing about would find out about her alter ego. But no, once they decided she was "Old Money"–a laugh, because, though she could put on a good show, she certainly didn't come from their kind of Old Money–they simply accepted her. She was not exactly of their level, but she was fun and a bit mysterious. That made her attractive enough to get her to all the places and people she needed to write about.

Life was good. Her salary rose slowly, like a flood on its way to topping the levee.

But then. There's always a "but then," isn't there? For Harriet, it was a car accident. She was returning along the coast from a solitary weekend getaway. In the fog and the dark, something happened, no one ever knew exactly what. She was found, her little sports car crumpled against a tree and halfway down a ravine. She was far from home, but close enough to a decent hospital. There was never a question of transferring her closer to LA. Far too much damage. On her, as well as the car.

Once doctors determined that she could be saved, they did what they could. The right side of her face was a mess. Her nose was broken, her cheekbone was crushed, even the bone around her eye was splintered along one edge. There were cuts and bruises everywhere. The left side of her face fared much better, showing abrasions and bruising, but no broken bones. The doctors called in a plastic surgeon to work on her face. The best, they said. The only, the nurses told her.

When she was finally awake enough to be rational, she signed a consent form for the surgery. She went into surgery hopeful, and came out shattered.

She was told later what happened. The surgeon, scalpel in hand, bent over her, too close, according to the surgical nurse. He pressed her damaged face here and there. He laughed. Then he swayed, and, ever so gracefully, slid to the floor. At first, they thought he had a heart attack. But as he collapsed, he dragged the scalpel down along the left side of her face, penetrating far enough to slice into the trigeminal nerve, and leaving a pathway of scar tissue down the left side of her face clear down to her jaw. That, and major nerve damage to her face. Irreparable.

Harriet had never heard of the trigeminal nerve, but she saw the devastation once she recovered. If one could call it recovery. They tried to repair the bone damage on the right, but there remained dents and scars, and a nose that was off-kilter just enough to make people clean their spectacles.

But on the other side, the side relatively untouched by the car accident, the scalpel damage left her with a drooping eye and a downturned mouth, as well as that long livid scar down the side of her face. The scar, which never went away, could be partially hidden with a waterfall of hair, if she chose, but there was all that other. The bruises healed, and so did the small cuts. But the visible damage to her face didn't. Harriet didn't think she ever would heal inside either.

She stayed away from Los Angeles. Away from the parties, away from the "friends," none of whom came to visit or call, away from everything. She even refused to see her editor, the only person she phoned to explain her absence. "Car accident," she said, never mentioning the horridly botched job from the drunk plastic surgeon. Her editor gave her a generous severance package, reluctant to see her leave her job.

She found out about the doctor's drinking problem from the nurses. They didn't realize he was such a closet drunk, a vice hidden from everyone. To Harriet, it sounded like no one ever saw him actually sober. A secret drunk whose drinking finally caught up to him on her watch.

She sued him, of course, begging her lawyer to confer with his lawyer, and spare her the need to confront the doctor in person. She had to visit the judge once, thankfully in his chambers alone, to prove the extent of the damage. Photos wouldn't be enough, she told the lawyer, as she drew a heavy veil across her face. When the judge saw the extent of the damage, he awarded her the full amount of restitution.

Harriet felt no pity when the surgeon was forced to sell his house, his cars, all his fancy trappings. His wife divorced him as well.

Harriet moved to New York, met Ed, and married him.

Of course, life didn't move so smoothly as that seems to imply. She did move to New York, where she took up where she left off. She found a job writing play reviews for another middle-market paper, but smaller than the California one. She could put on a veil, sit in a dark theater, and write up her assignment, all without anyone seeing her. She left Tilly behind in LA, and changed her name to Harriet Wright. Harriet Stevens of California morphed into Harriet Wright of New York City. Of course, no one would recognize her anyway, considering the changes. But she preferred to reinvent at least part of herself. Veils and hats were in fashion anyway, so, though her veil was much more substantial than most, she didn't look or feel out of place. For her, they added an air of mystery, and became her signature pieces.

That worked well until she wrote a scathing review of a play from a newcomer by the name of Edward Wright. "The playwright— the only recognizable positive being that word and the writer's name—apparently attempted to cobble together the lives of his lovers, meeting in some unnamed tropical locale, thrown into this dump of a resort by the hand of God. No other reason appeared." She ended the review by blasting, "Darling, it's been done, and monumentally better too. Check out *Casablanca*. Then, get a day job."

He sent her a letter, asking for a meeting. She demurred. He tracked her down. She avoided him. Somehow, he worked the receptionist at the paper just enough to discover when she'd deliver her next review. He also unearthed the detail that she wore hats pulled low, most with veiling hiding her face. That part, she didn't know.

He waited for her on the given day. Approached her so that she couldn't escape out the door. He was not obnoxious, not at all. She wondered why, considering his reputation for putting people off.

"I admire your writing," he said, apparently careful not to get too close and scare her into bolting past him. "I'm Ed Wright."

Harriet startled. She never met one of the writers she lambasted, and she hadn't lambasted many at all, actually. And none as scathingly as Ed Wright. It gave her pause. "Why should I talk to you?"

"I know, I know," he said. "You've hit my writing pretty hard."

"Your writing is..." Should she be kind? No. "Lousy."

His face lowered into thunder. But then, his look cleared and he surprised her by laughing. "It must be, to have you slice it to pieces like you did. I'd like to get better. You can make me a better writer."

She raised an eyebrow, though, she suddenly realized, he couldn't see it through the veil. She hadn't helped anyone with writing since college, when she...well, when she "re-wrote," or edited, if you wanted to beat around the bush.... In spite of herself, she was curious. Maybe she could... "Why me? I—" She allowed herself a pinch of intrigue.

He held up a hand. "I'm sure you think I'm crazy." She did. "But you're writing is to the point. Your reviews are honest, complete, good. Plus, we have the same last name."

She laughed. The pinch of intrigue increased to a full teaspoon. "As I recall, I told you to get another job."

Ed nodded. "You did. That's why I'm here. What other job should I get? I love the theater. Besides, your work–you–interest me."

Oh, stop this, Harriet told herself. *He may be good looking, but...* She took a closer peek from under her hat. Yes, he was that, even though he was shorter than she was. *But. For heaven's sake, Harriet, just let down your guard a bit. This isn't LA, and maybe I could help him. I'm a decent writer, that's for certain.* She wondered where this could conceivably go. With her damaged looks, he couldn't possibly be attracted to her...like that. Of course, while she was damaged on the outside, based on the way he treated everyone else, he must be damaged somehow on the inside.

She took herself in hand. She had work to do. "Look, I don't have time right now. I've got a play to review." *Let's see what he'll do with that.*

"'Right now?' How about later?" Ed asked.

Harriet was already shaking her head *no*, but it must have come off as *yes* somehow. Well, the *right now* part was *yes, right now.* But no, she wasn't sure about later, not with him. Cheeky devil. But persistent, she had to give him that.

"So, you have a play to review right now." Ed cocked his head. "How's about I come with you? I'll sit in silence, I promise."

Where does he think he's going with this? But Ed was smiling, and not trying to crowd her. She wasn't looking forward to this particular performance, having seen a play by the same author earlier in the year, and finding it inane. Well, perhaps Ed would be someone to listen to her throw barbs under her breath. Against her better judgment, she agreed. "Avalon theater, one o'clock. Be late, I won't wait." She watched his shoulders relax. "Now, if you'll excuse me." He stepped aside, and she strode off.

Over time, he turned out to be an amiable companion, never pushy, never expounding in the theater on what they were watching. He was a good listener. And he had a caustic wit.

Occasionally, she found herself asking permission to use some of the phrases he came out with.

Harriet wondered if Ed was blind, or at least, sight-impaired. He never commented on the hats pulled low, or the veils. She learned to laugh again, especially as he whispered a particular nasty—but true—comment on a scene or a turn of phrase.

One particularly warm day, they lingered in a nearby park after a performance. Harriet finished her scribbled notes and tucked the notebook away in her capacious purse. "That takes care of that. All I have to do it write it up. I wonder if you have any bon mots for me today."

"Have you known otherwise?" Ed said. "But today, it's more blatant than usual."

"Go ahead."

"Take off the veil."

Harriet stiffened. "I...I... No." She clenched her fists and brought her elbows in close to her sides. She couldn't look at Ed.

"You already told me you were in a car accident," Ed said. "How bad can it be? You can talk, you can laugh, you can tilt your head. What else could a person want?"

"What else? What else! Are you kidding? How about being able to walk down the street without people gaping at me? How about being able to put makeup on eyes that match? I'm not talking about the makeup matching. I'm talking about the *eyes* matching." She sputtered out, pinching her lips tight.

"So? I've been around you for weeks now, and I think you're wonderful. Why won't you take off the veil?"

"Are you crazy?" She missed the "wonderful" part completely. "I'm not showing this face to anybody." Her anger, never far from the surface, threatened to turn into a volcanic explosion.

"I don't care what you look like, Harriet." Ed's voice was low and soothing, but Harriet resisted.

"You'll care if I show you."

Ed stood up and looked around, swiveling like a ballerina marionette on a jewelry box. He seemed to peer into every tree, over every bush, down every path. It was a small park, and he returned to his seat. He touched her arm and said, "There's absolutely nobody around but me." He cleared his throat. "Look, Harriet, I don't care what you *look* like. I just like who you are."

Harriet's anger boiled over. *Once he sees me, I'll never see him again, so who cares if he tells everybody how horrid I look? They already know I'm weird.* She reached up and pulled off her hat, taking the veil with it. But she wouldn't turn her head toward him.

Ed slid off the bench and knelt in front of her. Ed being Ed, he said, "Wow! Your face really does look horrible!"

For some reason, every bit of Harriet's anger dissipated. She looked down at him. He had a hand raised, as if ready to stroke her face. But it was frozen mid-gesture. "So, I suppose you want to touch all my lovely scars now."

"Nope." He dropped his hands onto her knees, but never took his eyes from hers. He shrugged. "I gotta admit, I've never seen anyone with so many..."

"Scars," she said. "Go ahead and say it. You said worse already."

His face turned rose-red, flushing all at once. He moved to sit next to her again. His hand crept over to grasp one of hers. "I'm sorry, Harriet. You just took me by surprise, whipping off your hat like that." He pivoted to look directly at her.

She couldn't resist looking sideways at him, considerably easier with her cockeyed eye. "It really is pretty bad, isn't it?"

"Must've been a horrendous accident," he said. "But I'm glad you survived it."

She sent him a wry smile. "Sometimes I wonder..."

"You know, Harriet." He took a finger and rotated her face to his. "You are like an oyster."

She raised her eyebrows, at least, the one eyebrow she could control. "What? What are you talking about?"

"Yeah, an oyster. They're all gnarly and bumpy on the outside, and then you open them up and, voila!, a beautiful pearl. That's what you are. Your outside isn't so great. Well, just your face, you know. The rest of you is pretty...va-va-voom."

Harriet laughed. "That's the first time anyone told me that."

"It's true," Ed said. "But your inside's smooth and shiny, like a pearl."

"'Smooth and shiny'?" She shook her head. "You never were very good with words."

"I know, I know. You hated my play." He brightened. "But I'm working on another. Maybe you can help me get better."

Harriet considered. "That's possible." She realized they veered away from the subject of her face. A pleasant surprise.

"I've been waiting for this," Ed said.

"Waiting for what?"

"Waiting for you to trust me enough to show me your face."

"And?" Harriet had no idea where this conversation was going.

"I want you to be my pearl," Ed said.

"What on earth are you talking about?" Harriet did have an inkling of where Ed was headed, but she could feel turmoil building in her stomach. Nerves.

"Marry me, you crazy woman! My pearl, I want you to marry me, that's what I'm talking about!" He fell silent, watching her face.

Is this really happening? Harriet thought. "We haven't known each other very long—"

"I know that too," Ed said, "but I knew from the start that I wanted you. I don't care what you look like on the outside, I love your inside. That's far more important."

"Finally, you become eloquent," Harriet said. He never lied to her before. There was no reason to think he lied when he said that he loved her. It struck her that, strange as it was, she felt the same about him. She tried out a smile. She knew it was crooked, but she made sure to turn so she faced Ed fully.

Ed leaned in, ran his hand up through her hair and pulled her toward him.

Oh, dear God! Harriet hadn't kissed a man since before the accident. She started to panic, but then gave herself over to the moment. *Let's see if he really means it.* She felt his lips touch hers. One side was numb and felt nothing, but the other side registered a gentle touch, and she rose to it. His lips slid away to her ear. "Ah!" was all she could get out.

Ed enveloped her in an embrace and whispered, "I love you, my pearl."

She couldn't stop herself. Nor did she want to. "I love you too, Ed." She could feel tears coursing down her scarred cheeks.

"Do we need a ring?" Ed asked. "Or shall we just go to the justice of the peace right now?"

"Now?" She pulled back from him.

He was so radiant. "Yes, now! Right now!"

She stared at him. "Now? Really? Ed–"

"Give me one reason to wait. No, you can't come up with one, can you?"

He didn't give her time to think. But she realized, she didn't want to come up with a reason to say no. She sent out her crooked smile. "No, I can't. So...why not?"

Without a word, Ed grabbed her hands and pulled her to her feet. He drew her into an embrace and gave her another kiss. "You've made me the happiest man in the world," he whispered in her ear. "Let's go!"

Off they went, arms around each other, Harriet's hat and veil forgotten on the park bench.

In a flurry of activity, they pulled two strangers in from the court anteroom and tied the knot. The judge waived the 24-hour waiting period, and neither the judge nor the couple gave Harriet's face more than a cursory glance. Thus, Harriet Wright became Mrs. Ed Wright.

•   •   •

"So, that's my story, and I'm sticking to it," Harriet said, punctuating that with a nod and a waggle of one finger. "It's been interesting, I'll give you that, Lynn. But you're right, Ed does adore me. And the feeling's mutual."

"The best stories end with both parties happy, no matter how others might feel about it," Lynn said, knowing by now that Harriet was a realist, if nothing else, and wouldn't take offense. Everyone in New York knew Ed was difficult to work with. But they also knew that his wife was a sweetie, as well as a better than decent editor for Ed, and she, if no one else, could get him to do what was needed.

"You were right, Lynn," Harriet said, "I am exhausted. I think I'm going to turn in, if you don't mind."

"Not at all," Lynn said. "When the men return, I'll tell Ed you went off to bed."

"Thanks," Harriet said. She plucked up her coat and hat, and Ed's as well, from the clothes hooks. With a jaunty little finger wave, she left, closing the suite door behind her.

Lynn went around turning off all the lights but the ones over the beds. She went back to the window. In spite of the snow, the moon was just bright enough to cast a magic silver coating over the scenery, whenever it appeared between the scudding clouds.

She sighed, picked up her drink, and settled in the chair just vacated by Harriet. She danced the chair around with her toes to face the window. One last sip, and Lynn placed her glass on a nearby table.

Soon, her eyes drooped and she decided to turn in, rather than wait for Alfred to return. He would know instantly when he opened the door to their suite that she was in bed. He would send Ed back to Harriet. She snuggled down under the blankets and breathed a happy sigh. Alfred wouldn't keep her waiting long.

-5-

Before the Century reached Chicago the next morning, the Lunts and the Wrights spent breakfast watching out the dining car window, and commenting on the growing flurries. Though a bit apprehensive about the weather, they turned their attention to enjoying French omelets and slices of thick bacon. When they pulled into the station, it was still snowing. Even though the platform was protected indoors, they could hear the wind swirling around outside. They hustled two platforms over to board the Hiawatha, the train to Milwaukee. Alfred hung back a bit to watch the baggage being unloaded from the Century platform and trundled to the Hiawatha platform. All seemed in order when Lynn, shepherding the Wrights to the correct platform, turned to check on Alfred and their baggage. They stepped up and in, finding the carriage nowhere near full.

The conductor called "All aboard!" and the Hiawatha slid out of the station. They encountered falling snow again. She wondered how things were faring at the estate, then set the thought aside. *No sense worrying about something I can do nothing about,* she thought, and turned her attention to Alfred and their guests. The Century had treated them like royalty, and they all managed a good night's sleep, in spite of a late night round of cards for the men, in the club car, before retiring for the night. Even Ed didn't express anything negative. At least at that point.

Lynn was sure he would, considering the storm was picking up in speed and intensity. She steeled herself to remain calm.

Two hours later, they made one last change in Milwaukee, onto the small train headed, eventually, across the state. It would make a stop in Waukesha, then beyond, to deposit them in Genesee Depot, before continuing west.

Would Ed complain? Lynn held her breath. Sure enough, on the way to Genesee Depot, Ed was uncomfortable and impatient. He shuffled around on the seat, tucking his camel hair coat around his thighs. He frowned, got up, pulled the coat tight around him and sat down again, making sure the coat would protect his backside. "Is it always this cold in Wisconsin?" He wrapped his white airman's scarf around his neck, burying his chin. The Century from New York was toasty warm, almost too much so, and so was the Hiawatha to Milwaukee, but this train seemed to assume everyone came with their own personal internal furnace.

"It *is* winter, dear," Harriet said.

"Yeah, but New York is never this cold," Ed said.

Alfred chuckled. "Of course it is. But this is, I'll admit, a rather unusual winter, or at least this weather is."

"And New York streets are just as windy," Lynn said. "You certainly bundle up when you walk out, don't you, Ed?"

"Walk? I never walk anywhere. I hail a taxi, dash for the door, and insist on being dropped practically *in* the lobby."

The other three laughed, but Ed appeared to be serious.

"I'm glad you came with us." Lynn attempted to turn the conversation. No better way than to stroke Ed's ego a bit.

"I am too," Harriet said. "I've heard so much about your getaway." She turned to look out the window. "Too bad we can't see more through the storm."

"We'll put you up in the cottage," Alfred said. "It's up the hill from the main house. Not very far. Even with drifts, you should be able to make your way down for meals. You'll have plenty of privacy. We can get going on those rewrites before the others get here."

Privacy, yes, thought Lynn. *That and plenty of space to get a lot done. Better yet, it keeps Ed out of our hair for a little while every day.* Not that she didn't like Ed. He was terribly talented. And his wife was a delight. She thought of Harriet's amber hair in a stylish lift above her face. Her pale green eyes, like peridot, provided another worthy distraction. She was an attractive woman. She was soft-spoken and honest, though more often kept her own counsel and let Ed take the lead. Harriet had a bearing that spoke of confidence in herself, flaws and all.

The train pulled out of the Milwaukee station, heading for Genesee Depot, where a driver waited for them. At least, Lynn hoped their driver was waiting. The snowstorm seemed to be picking up more force, although that was perhaps due to the speed of the train and the wind swirling around.

"So, this cottage," Ed said, his tone condescending. "Does it have indoor plumbing?"

Alfred looked at Lynn and sent her a deep laugh. That, and a look that said, *Shall we have some fun with him?*

Lynn didn't even have to shake her head to send Alfred a negative response, they could read each other so well. "Yes, Ed, indoor plumbing, running water, and a furnace. Ben, our caretaker, will have the heat up in both houses."

"Dear," Harriet said, touching Ed on the sleeve, "we are not going on an Antarctic expedition."

"Might as well be," Ed growled. "Might as well be with Scott on that doomed expedition to the North Pole."

"South Pole, dear." Harriet's voice was just barely loud enough to be heard by all.

"Either way, we'll be stuck out here in the middle of nowhere," Ed said.

"The better to get the work done," Alfred said, reflecting Lynn's thoughts exactly.

They settled into a silence broken only by the sound of the wheels on the rails, with the wind providing background percussion.

By the time they arrived at the small depot, Lynn's feet, in spite of her galoshes, were chilled to the bone. None of them removed coats, or even hats, on the ride out from Milwaukee. They stayed on the train and watched as the local trainmaster helped unload all of the baggage. With everything stacked neatly under the station's overhang, they stood and pulled their coats tighter around themselves. They added fur-lined gloves, drew their hats even lower, and hurried to exit the train.

To Lynn's great relief, Ben, their caretaker and driver, met them on the platform.

"Hurry up, folks," he called. "I left the car running." He hustled to grab suitcases and hatboxes from his four charges, and set off for the car. The others hefted the remaining pieces and followed Ben through the station.

"Another hour on the road, I suppose," Ed said, as they walked.

"No, no," Lynn said, "just a few miles or so up the road. Come on, let's go!" She picked up the pace as she emerged into the storm. Ben, waiting for her, led her, followed by the others, to the waiting car. Though the roads looked almost impassable, it was the "almost" that should save them.

They slogged along, piled luggage into the trunk, and slid into the car. "Pretty wicked storm," Ben said, pulling out of the station and heading down the road. "They say it's going to go on like this for a few more days."

"Great." A grunt from Ed.

"I came close to bringing the tractor and the haywagon," Ben quipped, "but I didn't think your guests would appreciate riding in the open air."

Alfred and Ben shared a laugh that segued off into a matching howling gust from the wind.

"The railroad kept the area around the station fairly open," Ben said, struggling with the wheel as the wind played with the car. "But I don't know how long they can keep up."

"Do you think the train can get through tomorrow?" Lynn asked. She sat wedged between Ben and Alfred in the front seat, a hatbox on her lap. She slid under Alfred's arm laid across the back of the seat, and tried to make herself as narrow as possible, in order to give Ben enough elbow room to maneuver.

Ben nodded. "As long as the plows can keep up, we'll be okay. But I don't know about tomorrow night, or even in the afternoon. They reckon the storm's just giving us a preview today. It'll ease off a bit, but then it's going to kick up again. Oh! The wife says to tell you the stove is still out. Sorry we couldn't get to that before we knew you were coming."

"Don't worry about us, Ben," Lynn said. She flung her next words over her shoulder, being hardly able to fully turn around. "Harriet and Ed, come down to the main house for meals. No kitchen facilities up there at the cottage. So sorry!"

Harriet leaned forward and said, "Not to worry. We can slog through the snow. It's not that far, is it?"

"Not at all," Lynn assured them. "There are always Wellington boots in the back hall up there, so feel free to use them."

Harriet said, "We'll be fine. Thanks!"

"How about the animals?" Alfred asked Ben, always concerned with all the goings-on of the farm, especially the animals. "Is the barn strong enough?"

"That barn could hold off the Wicked Witch of the West," Ben said. The car fishtailed a bit as they approached the road heading out of town toward the estate. Ben fought to keep the car on the straightaway. "Good thing we've got woods along here. Decent windbreak."

Lynn leaned into Alfred. "Leave him alone now, Alfred. He needs to concentrate on the road."

Alfred nodded. "We're almost there. I don't know how he can see where he's going. I hope he can make it home all right."

Lynn took Alfred's hand and squeezed. She hoped her fear wouldn't radiate through her fingers into Alfred's. She could hear Harriet mumbling in the backseat, presumably prayers to whomever she thought the patron saint of...what? Safe travel, perhaps? Maybe snowstorms. Lynn felt a giggle building, but a look out past the furiously working windshield wipers squashed that pretty quickly. She pressed her eyes shut and hoped.

Before long, Lynn felt herself tilting a bit into Ben as the car tiptoed around the corner into their driveway. She took a deep breath and opened her eyes. She couldn't see the house at first, not until Ben eased down the driveway, staying close to the stone retaining wall as a reference point. They lumbered into the courtyard at Ten Chimneys without more than a few slips and slides.

The L-shape of the house embraced a lovely courtyard framed with a low wall made of local boulders, creating a haven of sorts with a massive oak tree in the middle, though the wall was close to being obscured by drifts. The wrought iron gate at the entrance was open and frosted with globs and sweeps of snow. The tree, and even the upper stories of the house, looked like ghosts behind the swirling and sweeping blizzard. Though it was only mid-afternoon, the sky promised no sun at all, and the light, such as it was, struggled to deny it was night, it was almost that dark. The courtyard itself was putting up a brave fight to keep the snow depth to a reasonable level. But it was a losing battle.

As Ben maneuvered around the tree, Lynn watched the familiar rise of the land along the right of the house, burying the bottom story. From the courtyard, the house had three substantial stories, the bottom one graced by a portico which protected the two separate doors leading into the house. Ben pulled the car up as close to the portico as he could before getting out to unload the luggage while Lynn unlocked the laundry room door and shepherded him, and the luggage, into the warm house.

"I'll ride up to the cottage with Ed and Harriet," Alfred called from the car. "Ben can bring me back down before he goes home. I'll remind Ed and Harriet to come down to the main house for meals."

Lynn waved her understanding. She closed the outside door to the laundry room and shed her coat, shaking off the snow. She stomped her boots and levered them off. Her hat had a second toque of white on top of the mink one she donned when leaving New York. She opened the door and flicked it off outside.

She sent up a fervent prayer of thanks to Ben for bringing the heat up to a comfortable level in the house and the cottage. And for surely filling the refrigerators in both kitchens. She did a quick check of the laundry room, then opened the door to the foyer and main staircase, and listened for the reassuring pings and ticks of the radiators. She retreated and checked that the coat rack in the laundry room contained plenty of hangers for their coats, and the coats of the others when they arrived the next day. Weather permitting. She crossed her fingers.

Alfred soon appeared and she pulled him indoors. They watched Ben struggle to reverse himself and retreat from the courtyard, in case he needed assistance. But the car, headlights providing only minimal guidance, fishtailed a bit as Ben brought the car around to head out the gate. The engine gunned a bit stronger and the car forced its way out and down the drive. Though they couldn't discern taillights, they did hear as the car turned onto the country road. Ben was on his way. Home was close, and Lynn knew he would be fine from here.

Alfred went through the same sequence Lynn did. He slipped outside under the portico and shook off his coat without taking it off. He stamped his feet, then rushed into the laundry room, slamming the door shut behind him. "The heat's on! Rejoice, rejoice!" Alfred crowed. He pried off his boots, shed his coat and situated all where they wouldn't drain meltwater in too large an area.

Alfred shook his shoulders and faced Lynn across their suitcases. They both began to laugh.

"Oh, darling," Lynn said, "I wondered if we'd ever get Ed and Harriet out here in one piece. How does she put up with him?"

"A rhetorical question if I ever heard one," Alfred said. "I wonder what people say about us?"

"That we are a perfect match," Lynn said. "We are, aren't we? And that is *not* a rhetorical question. Let's go upstairs. We'll deal with Ed and Harriet later."

~6~

Lynn, having unpacked upstairs and changed into a flannel nightgown covered by a heavy brocade dressing gown, was sitting in the drawing room of the main house, listened to the storm outside. She sat as close to the fire as she could, extending her long elegant fingers to heat them. Curled up in the coral velvet chair closest to the fireplace, she hunched her shoulders and rubbed her hands together. She was no longer cold inside, as she was in New York. She and Alfred weren't back in Wisconsin often in the winter, and this was simply weather-cold, nothing more. But though the house was actually pleasantly warm, with Lynn being British, anything slightly leaning toward cold didn't suit her very well. Even in the summer, she hired local boys to come in and build a fire in the fireplace, no matter what room she perched in. But this was winter in Wisconsin, and it was bitter outside. She needed a conflagration to keep warm.

"Here, Lynnie." Alfred proffered one of the two glass mugs of steaming amber liquid.

"Oh, darling! A hot toddy. Just what I ordered," Lynn said, turning from the fire for a moment to take the mug and wrap her hands around it. She tucked her feet up under her again, and settled back in the chair.

Watching her husband, handsome in the velveteen smoking jacket she fitted and sewed for him, Lynn marveled again at the man she married twenty-five years before. Because every woman he met seemed to fall in love with him, backstage was always a challenge as he would weave around and among his female cohorts. Lynn, following in his wake, found it distressing at first. *Those big brown eyes. Like falling into a vat of gourmet chocolate,* Lynn mused. *And I love chocolate.*

"What you ordered was summer, Miss Fontanne," Alfred said, bringing her out of her reverie. "Sorry I couldn't deliver on that one. The drink and the fire will have to do." He went to the blue velvet settee on the wall opposite the fireplace and stretched, half-reclining.

Lynn craned to look out the window. Miles and miles away from New York streetlights, the night here had little to offer beyond the soft rectangles of light sputtering out from the windows. "Pull the drapes, will you, darling?" She smiled. She knew she was baiting him. "Oh wait, Mr. Lunt. You can't. You wouldn't let me buy enough fabric to draw them." She sipped her drink and murmured, "Half-Curtain Alf," just loud enough so he could catch it.

Alfred seemed to ignore her dig. He set his drink on the nearby table and groaned as he stretched. "I wonder how Ed and Harriet are doing up in the cottage."

Lynn said, "I'm sure he's up there now, working his heart out. Maybe he's ready for a little breather. Shall we call them down?"

Alfred laughed, recognizing her light sarcasm. "You're not serious, surely. I'm not about to disturb Ed now that we've got him out of the glitz and glamor of New York. Too many distractions for them both. Harriet can just look sideways at him, and he's got his coat on, ready for another party."

"You're right. We can check on his progress tomorrow. I know we gave him plenty of marginalia on the script to look at. That should keep him busy. I hope he takes your suggestions to heart." She didn't sound very sure of that last part. Ed Wright, Famous Playwright, was not known for his flexibility. He wrote what he wrote, and that was it. He didn't take kindly to suggestions to revise.

"Maybe we should call Harriet and invite her down for a drink? Lure her away? Maybe she'd welcome a trek through the snow. Or at least see how she's doing."

Alfred laughed. "Actually, that's not a bad idea. Give her a break from the impresario." He headed off for the telephone in the kitchen, but he was back in a flash. "The line's dead, Lynnie. Can't raise the operator at all."

"No distractions then. Perhaps it'll be back up tomorrow." She blew on her mug. "Harriet will have to carry on by herself, poor dear."

The thump of a log falling distracted them both. Alfred raced to the hearth and grabbed the tongs to wrestle the wayward log back onto the rack. They watched the sparks flare up the chimney. "Ah, well. It's neither here nor there," Lynn said. "We'll have all day tomorrow with the Wrights."

Alfred closed the firescreen and went to the window. "Good lord! Ullr, the god of winter, has made an appearance! Come look at this! You'd think Mother Nature used up all her snow in that blizzard in 1940, but it looks like '47 is going to be even worse."

Lynn set her empty mug on the hearth and joined Alfred at the window. She linked her arm in his and peered out. "I can see why the telephone lines are down. Look at the terrace! The snow's almost up to the top of the wall."

"Good thing we took the early train out. I wonder if the tracks will be cleared enough to get the others here tomorrow?" Alfred snorted. "Serves them right if they have to camp out in that windy Milwaukee depot." He pulled Lynn up into a hug and kissed her hair. "Plus, we have the essentials right here."

"If you mean me, I accept the compliment," Lynn said.

"I really meant Ed," Alfred said. "Harriet and you are just ornamentations."

Lynn slipped from his embrace and went to lean against the door jamb. She hooded her eyes and gazed at Alfred. "Well, either way, I'm for bed. If you come with me, it'll be the other warm place in this house."

It didn't take Alfred but a moment to bank the fire and follow her.

~7~

The next day, the phone lines were back up long enough for the stationmaster to call Ten Chimneys and warn them that trains were running late, very late. Ben, the Lunts' driver and estate manager, arrived at the estate to pick up Lynn and go to the station to pick up the rest of the party coming out from New York, but ended up sitting at the kitchen table with a cup of coffee, hoping the phone lines would hold until they could get notice of the train's arrival.

With the temperature plummeting and the snow continuing to fall, tension was increasing minute by minute when the phone rang.

Lynn jumped at the jangling and Alfred leaped to grab the receiver. "Yes? Yes, we'll be right–" Alfred frowned and set the receiver back on the cradle. "We got cut off. The lines must be down for good this time."

"We'd better set off," Lynn said.

Ben set his cup down, stood and reached for his jacket. "We'll get back as quick as we can, Mr. Lunt." He set off down the back stairs.

Alfred put his hands on Lynn's shoulders. "I really think you should let Ben go down alone to pick them up at the station," Alfred said, his forehead crinkled with worry. "I hate to see you go out in this weather."

"It's fine, Alfred." Lynn pulled on her gloves, then patted him on the chest. She was armored to the hilt against the cold. Long fur coat, one of Alfred's hats with earflaps, galoshes.

"I'd go with you, but I'm in the middle of cooking."

"Tush, Alfred. I promised to meet them, and that's what I'll do. Norma and I know each other, and I know she'll feel better if she sees someone she recognizes. Don't you worry. Ben will get us back in a jiffy."

Alfred followed her down the stairs to the back door. He leaned over and planted a kiss on her forehead. "Do take care, dear. I'd hate to lose you in the storm."

"Just keep the food warm, please," Lynn said. Hearing the car horn toot from the courtyard, she went to the door and, with a final wave to Alfred, plunged out into the wind and jumped in the car next to Ben.

With a bit of smooth driving, Ben had them out of the courtyard and down the drive.

So far, so good. The roads were still relatively visible, and, in spite of the blowing snow, they made good time going into town.

Once at the station, they pulled up as close as they dared under the deep overhang marking the entrance to the waiting room. "I'll run in and wait for them inside," Lynn told Ben. "You keep the car running. And the heater, please! I think I hear the train coming along." She was lucky enough to be on the leeward side of the car, so she could get out and slam the door without the wind taking it out of her hands. She ran for the shelter of the station.

She was just in time to see her guests disembark, grab coat collars and hoist suitcases, and run across the platform and into the depot.

The four travelers looked both tired and a bit disheveled. They shook off snow and began a stream of astonishment at the weather outside. Then Lynn waved at Norma, catching her attention.

"There! You see? I told you they promised a driver." Norma set down her suitcase. "And looks who's here to meet us." She went to

Lynn and encompassed her in a bear hug. "You are a sight for sore eyes. The others were afraid no one would be here to meet us. But I reassured them that you never let me down before."

"Truth be told," Lynn said, "we were a bit worried that the train wouldn't get here at all tonight. But here you are! I'm simply delighted." She turned to the others. "But we mustn't stand here gabbing. Ben is outside keeping the car warm."

Norma took Lynn's elbow. "A quick introduction. My husband, and thank you for inviting him along." Norma, a 60-plus actress, came eye-to-eye with her towering husband, both of them wrapped to the ears with coats and scarves. Her full-length sable coat and Cossack hat pulled as low as she could get it still didn't hide her red nose, though that was all that was showing. Even her eyes were shadowed under the fur hat.

Lynn nodded to each in turn. The two other girls acknowledged her with bobs of their heads, then turned to check that they had everything. In the shuffling, Lynn overheard a whispered exchange between Norma and her husband.

Norma's husband mumbled something about "Damn fine way to greet guests," and "New York wasn't–". She drew herself up and planted herself in front of him. Of the others, she was the one who knew Alfred and, more intimately, Lynn, though Norma had never visited Ten Chimneys. "Shush now," she whispered. "We're here. Lynn and Alfred take care of their own, and that includes us." She apparently smoothed his ruffled feathers, and, in response, he jammed his gloved hands into his pockets and nodded, whispering, "I know, dear, I know." But he said aloud, "I'm just tired."

"And hungry!" Lily, one of the young women actresses, added. She hunched her shoulders and fell silent. Although she had on a long wool coat, it appeared not to be enough to protect her completely. She turned up the collar that was drooping and held it tight against her throat. Her scarf, wrapped in a turban around her head, left her face exposed. She was not smiling.

Ellen, the other young actress, went across to Lily and stood close, as if to share body heat. Lily, taller by more than a head, might radiate more heat if Ellen could position herself just right. "We really should be wearing boots," she said. "Mine are packed. I didn't expect such foul weather, did you?"

Lily looked down at Ellen and shook her head. "My boots are packed too. When we left New York, it wasn't snowing, and we haven't had a moment in between trains to get them out. My feet are frozen!"

"I know," Ellen answered. "I think my hair is frozen. Even that dash from the train into the depot here chilled me to the bone. I don't think I've ever heard wind like that."

As if in a sympathetic response, the wind dropped away, exposing the sound of the car rumbling in wait outside. Everyone went to the door and peered out. Lynn waved to Ben, who got out and sprinted into the depot.

"From New York, right, Miss Fontanne?" He barely waited for her nod before he swept up a couple of suitcases and ushered them out the door. "I'm Ben, the Lunts' driver. Let's get you out of here before the storm gets worse."

Lynn watched Norma exchange glances of horror with the others, as if saying, "Worse? Where on earth are we, the Arctic?"

Ben managed to stuff everybody into the Ford, with luggage piled on laps and jammed in the trunk. No time, in this weather, for small talk. Once settled, they simply pulled into themselves, keeping collars turned up and hats turned down. Not much remained visible, other than a nose or two, and eyes shaded under hat brims. The rising shriek of the wind precluded any conversation anyway.

Ben slammed the trunk cover down, and checked the doors. Hopefully, nothing would fall out on the short trip out to the estate. If it did, it might be lost forever, passengers included. What a storm! *Here we go again*, Lynn thought, recalling the harrowing drive up to Ten Chimneys the day before.

A snowplow pulled in to the depot yard and swung around to stand chuffing just in front of the car destined for Ten Chimneys. The driver stepped down, slammed the door shut without turning off the engine, and ran to the car waiting behind his truck. Lynn hoped the snowplow would lead them home.

"I'm making one last run, Ben. Heading up to the Lunts' place, are you?" The driver noticed Lynn crammed in next to Ben. "Evenin', Miss Fontanne. It's a real howler out here." He had to holler to be heard. "Let's get you home. Follow me, Ben."

They set out from the depot, negotiating roads not improved even one jot from the day before. In fact, the area in front of the depot was filling up fast. The wind seemed determined to pack snow into every corner and crevice. There was certainly more than enough to go around, though Mother Nature continued to dump even more out of the clouds that hung low over the village.

It was a desperate run indeed, as the giant wet flakes continued to fall, clinging to everything as if to drown it in white. The windshield wipers proved almost ineffective, but Ben followed the plow closely, and managed to stay on the road. They passed the plow's garage at the volunteer fire department, and Lynn could imagine the driver thinking longingly of that home base. She didn't dare spare a glance in that direction, as if her inattention, not Ben's, risked them veering or sliding off the road. Still a few miles to go.

With heroic effort, both vehicles pulled down the driveway and into the Lunts' courtyard. The plow, after maneuvering to turn around, stood huffing and chugging, waiting for Ben to follow it out again. Ben deposited his passengers as close to the front door as he could, and struggled to unload the baggage.

"Get home and stay there," Alfred called to Ben over the wind's howls.

"That's it, Mr. Lunt," Ben said, swinging the last of the suitcases out of the back and setting them under the portico. "Supposed to snow all night. A real doozy of a storm."

"Darling," Lynn, standing under the portico, called over the wind, concern clear in her voice.

"Yes, dear?"

"Get inside. Let Ben get home. The road conditions are horrible." She turned an apologetic face to their guests already waiting in the foyer and shrugged, though not much of that showed underneath her mink coat. More flakes blew onto her hat, and hung suspended on the fur as if creating a halo.

A moment later, Ben was gone, and everyone, along with their baggage, was indoors, the front door tightly shutting out the weather. They moved from the foyer into the adjoining laundry room. They shook off coats and hats, spraying clouds of white. They levered off galoshes, shivering and laughing at the weather, now that they were indoors. Soon the coats were hung, sleeves and hems dripping. The galoshes stood underneath, sluicing their own water onto a braided rug that would, before too long, be soaked.

Once she took off her gear, Lynn went to Norma and gave her hug. "It is so wonderful to see you again, especially here at Ten Chimneys. Too bad it's in the winter when we can't get outside. We must remedy that come summer."

Lynn was taken by Norma's choice of clothing, some of it quite out of date, other parts perhaps way ahead of the curve. Her dress, silk, from the sway and shine of it, was of a fashionable length, certainly: mid-calf. But where the modern style called for a wasp-waist, Norma's dress flowed full from her neckline, with barely an indentation at the waist. The delightful colors– blues, lavenders and pale greens–ebbed into each other, like a Monet painting. The diaphanous fabric reminded Lynn of summer. But that was saved by a cream cardigan sweater, almost as long as the dress, with small pearl buttons marching up the front. The long, bell-like sleeves would cover Norma's fingers, if she didn't have them turned up a bit, revealing a bit of the dress sleeves.

But it was the scarves that enchanted Lynn. Not just one, not just two, but three swooped their way around Norma's neck and across her shoulders. One with purple iris almost obscuring the silver-gray background color. One with raucous red poppies splashed hither and yon on a cream base. And the third, the most vivid, looked as if a master painter cleaned his brushes on it. Reds, blues, greens, purples, oranges... Lynn could hardly see where one rich color blended into another. It practically shouted to be noticed.

"I see you like my attire," Norma said to Lynn. "I find that a collection of scarves can become head coverings, or even a skirt if they're large enough." She lifted the end of one scarf. "When I was just starting in the business, I needed something to make me stand out from the flock. So many girls, so much beauty. I took to flaunting my scarves. Don't know if it got me any roles, but they couldn't forget me, at least." She chuckled.

"You're right," Lynn said, "I do love the look. You bring a bit of summer into the cold."

"Oh, don't worry. I'm not dressing this way all week. Even if I am a California girl, I do know how to dress for the weather." She put a hand to her cheek, as if imparting a secret. "I brought long underwear."

"Me too," Norma's husband said. "Ready for any temperature."

The two young actresses blushed, while the others shared a laugh.

"Let's get you all settled. Come up the back stairs," Lynn said, "and bring your suitcases into the kitchen. I'll show you up to your rooms while Alfred dishes up some of his beef stew. It's getting late."

Norma and her husband followed by the two young women, hoisted their suitcases and clattered up to the kitchen behind Lynn and Alfred.

Norma Winter and her husband, Tate Alexander, were invited because Norma was playing a rather major role in the Lunts' latest Broadway play, to open in the fall, God willing and a good rewrite of the script by Ed Wright. Tate, a tall man with sandy hair sprinkled with silver, was along for the ride.

Ellen Lang and Lily Tremayne, the two young women—"girls," according to Alfred—were currently being mentored by the Lunts. Lynn was told the girls knew of each other, but, as far as Lynn knew, their relationship was based on having roles in the forthcoming play, not on a previous friendship. One had been working in Boston, the other in New York. It looked like a good beginning, however, as they seemed at ease with each other.

Once in the kitchen, Lynn said, "Alfred, be a dear and pour four whiskeys, will you? They'll need a bit of fortification in a moment."

"Whiskey and beef stew coming up," Alfred said, "whenever you're ready."

Lynn blew him a kiss and, like a mother duck, led her charges out of the kitchen, through the dining room and into a smaller reception room.

"Good God, Lynn!" Norma exclaimed. "I feel like I'm in a French farce! There are what—1, 2, 3... You've got too many doors here." She threw the end of a scarf over her shoulder.

"I know," Lynn said. "Isn't it fun? That's why we call this little room the flirtation room." She went into her actress stance. "Here behind me, as you see, are the doors to the dining room, which we just exited. Here, to the right, the main staircase goes down to the formal front door, where you came in. But we sneaked you up the back stairs to the kitchen." She gestured. "To my left, the stairway up to the bedrooms, where we're going now."

"Wait!" Tate set his suitcase down. "I forgot my briefcase in the kitchen." He strode off through the dining room doors.

"Hope you can find your way back," Norma called after him. She walked to a window past the doorway to the main staircase. "What's out here?"

"That window looks over the courtyard. Perhaps, in spite of the snowstorm, you can see the red cottage on the hill across the lawn, where Harriet and Ed are staying," Lynn said. "Behind you is the drawing room. So, if you come down from the bedrooms and turn left—"

"You'll be lost for sure," Tate said, coming back from the kitchen, briefcase in hand.

"No, you won't," Lynn said. "We'll be working in the drawing room, which is there on the left, so you just come downstairs from the bedrooms and turn left. Of course, come into the dining room and eat breakfast first." She watched everyone shake their heads, as if trying to settle the map of the house into place.

"For heaven's sake, how many stairs do you have in this house?" Norma asked.

Lynn let out a peal of laughter. "I always tell guests that our levels have levels. Because the house is built on a slope, it all depends on which door you come in as to what floor you're on."

Norma turned to her husband. "Tate, go back to the kitchen and ask Alfred for some bread crumbs. Or tie a string to a doorknob someplace."

"What's that, at the end of the…the flirtation room?" This time, it was Lily, one of the two "girls."

"Oh, there's a little hall with a bathroom off of it, and then there's what we call the yellow room at the end. That room is eternally cold, so we don't use it when the weather is bad. We always keep the door closed."

"That's it, then?" Tate said. "No more 'levels'?"

"Well, only if you count the library," Lynn said. "You can get to that by going up a few steps from the drawing room." Norma groaned. "Or from that cold hallway." She waggled her finger at the far door. "Everything is connected."

Norma puffed out a breath of air. "And here's me, with no sense of direction whatsoever." She flapped her hand at Lynn. "Don't worry. I'll get it by the end of the week."

Lynn smiled. "You'll have no trouble at all, Norma. But let's go upstairs. You can drop off your bags and then we'll get some nice warm food into you."

They set off up the stairs to the bedroom level.

"Here, Lily." Lynn opened a door directly to the right at the top of the stairs. "You'll have plenty of room in here. You're tall, and the bed is long enough to accommodate you."

Lily stepped in and set her suitcase on the bed.

"Norma and Tate, you're in the room just down the hall, on the left, if you'd like to take a peek. I'll be right there, as soon as I get the girls situated." The couple headed down the hall, and Ellen followed Lynn into Lily's room.

The room was spacious, done up in wallpaper with small sprays of rose and salmon flowers and a dramatic drape of fabric to match above the headboard. With several windows, it would be a light and airy room, once spring came around again. If it ever did.

"There's a luggage rack just over there, near the sofa." Lynn pointed across the room. "That'll give you a little extra room to unpack and spread out."

"I get a desk and a sofa," Lily said. "*And* a fireplace! Luxury, for certain." She shifted her suitcase to the luggage rack, snapped open the latches, and threw back the top to reveal a plaid flannel nightgown.

"Ah! Ever the practical young lady!" Lynn said. "I see you are a girl after my own heart. There is simply nothing like a long flannel nightshirt for a brazenly cold winter night."

"I came prepared for almost anything," Lily said, reaching in to pull out a pair of thick wool socks.

"Smart girl," Lynn said. "Feel free to make use of the Bombay chest against the wall. We'll be here a week, so you might as well be comfortable."

Lily took out her nightgown and held it to her chest. She straightened up to survey the room. "This will do just fine. It's beautiful." She turned to Lynn. "Thank you for inviting us."

Lynn said, "I'm so glad you and Ellen were able to join us. Alfred and I can help you two—" she gestured to Ellen standing just inside the doorway "—get your roles firmed up and ready. In the meantime, make yourself comfortable. "Ellen, your room is down at the end of the hall, beyond a bathroom between your two bedrooms." She pointed to a door in Lily's room. "It's right through there. Lily, Ellen has access only from the hall, but I think you two girls can share?" It really wasn't much of a question, but simply a polite way of inviting acceptance.

"Of course, Miss Fontanne." Ellen and Lily laughed at their responses said almost in unison.

"Ellen, come along. I'll show you your room." Lynn moved down the hallway and pointed out the bathroom as they passed. "Unfortunately, as you see, you do not have an adjoining door, as Lily does. But as you said, you'll figure out a good way to make it work."

Lily called out from her room. "I can only see the roof from here. And it's still snowing! Is it always like this?"

Lynn tilted her chin at Ellen. "That does not deserve an answer. It's winter." She leaned in to whisper, "We're not here much in the winter anyway. New York is usually cozier." Lynn shepherded Ellen into the end room, where she disappeared around a corner.

Before Lynn followed Ellen, she looked into the bedroom door to the left. "Mr. Alexander and Norma, here you are. I hope you'll be comfortable as well. I'll check on Ellen and be right back."

"Please," Tate said, "call me Tate."

Lynn sent him a sparkling look. "Of course. Tate. Thank you. We're delighted that you were able to get away from the accounting firm for a while to join us out here in the wilds. I hope that we don't talk too much theater for you."

"Not to worry. I brought a few cases and resources I need to study. When Norma and you folks are wrapped up in lines and scenes, I will make myself scarce," Tate said. His grin revealed dimples and lit up his eyes.

Lynn was enchanted. She turned and stepped into Ellen's room. Considerably smaller than the one Lily would inhabit, Ellen's room was, nevertheless, delightful, partly due to the explosion of cabbage roses on the wallpaper, and partly due to the little alcove cradling the head of the small bed. No room for desk or sofa, yet it had a handsome chest of drawers, as well as a number of small closets. Intimate and cozy. Perfect for Ellen's diminutive size.

Ellen set her suitcase down and clapped her hands, clearly enchanted. "I feel like I've walked into a summer garden. This room will do a lot to alleviate the cold."

"I'm happy you like it," Lynn said. "It's one of my favorites. You have wall sconces on each side of the bed, so you can read in bed, if you wish."

"I will wish, I'm sure," Ellen said. "Cuddle up under the comforter and study the scenes Mr. Wright churns out." She hugged herself and walked to the window. She let out a whoop. "Lily's right. The weather is still lousy. I can barely see the red house up the hill. I've got a good view of the courtyard, though. When the wind isn't blowing everything out of sight, at least."

"That's the cottage you can see," Lynn told Ellen. "By the way, the door here leads to a bathroom adjoining Miss Winter's and Mr. Alexander's room, but we'll leave that one for them, as long as you're willing to pop down the hall and share the other one with Lily."

Ellen nodded. "Quite willing, Miss Fontanne. I'm sure we'll have no trouble."

Lynn nodded. "I'm just going to check on the others." She slipped out Ellen's door and returned to Norma and Tate's room.

"The room is perfect, Lynn," Norma said. "Lots of windows and a fireplace. And a chair for lounging."

"We put you in here, because it has the biggest bed. Lily's bed is big enough for two, but it's only a full-size. This one is a true double."

"I'm grateful," Norma said. "Tate and I are not the smallest of people, tall and a bit...um, wide, shall we say?" They all chuckled.

"By the way, Tate, I wouldn't recommend the desk," Lynn said. "For someone as tall as you are, it would be a bit undersized. We have plenty of other areas for you to work."

Tate chuckled. "Truly, I was wondering a bit. I don't think my knees would fit under."

Lynn said, "I hope you really will be fine with us so busy with the play. We won't have much time to entertain you."

Norma snuggled up to her husband, and he looked down at her with clear affection. "No need to worry about Tate, Lynn," she said. "He's used to fending for himself when my acting takes precedence." Her honey-brown eyes sparkled. She reached up to reset the combs holding her thick brown hair away from her face.

Lynn found her beauty subtle, rather than striking. A few years older than Lynn's fifty-nine years, Norma clearly knew how to use makeup and hairstyle to her advantage. She was a good actress, and few could hold a candle to her stage presence, even at her age. *We were lucky to get her*, Lynn thought, *at any age.* "Well, we shouldn't keep Alfred's stew waiting," Lynn said. "After fighting your way out here, you deserve something to warm your bones."

"I seem to recall you ordering whiskey as well." Norma's face flashed with humor. "Right now, that may work quicker than the stew."

"I'm with you, dear," Tate put in. "But I've heard kudos for Alfred's cooking, so I'm not about to throw a shadow on that by asking for whiskey first."

Lynn said, "A diplomat among us. Perfect. Alfred gets a bit testy if we don't go into swoons over even his simplest vegetables. Heaven only knows what he'd do if you turn your nose up at his beef stew."

They shared a chuckle.

Ellen appeared in the room. "There's a bathroom right there for you." She indicated the open door that led from their bedroom into the adjoining bathroom. "There's a door to my room too."

"Oh, yes," Lynn said. "But we'll reserve that one for Miss Winter and Mr.—Tate." She turned to Norma. "Just lock the door that would let you through to Ellen's room, and you may use that bathroom exclusively for the two of you. That makes so much better sense."

"Lily and I will have no problem sharing the other bathroom, Miss Winter," Ellen said. Lily came up behind her and nodded.

"Please," Norma said. "Call me Norma, all of you. Miss Winter—Norma Winter—is my stage name. Mrs. Alexander is a bit too unwieldy for the stage, and Tate understands. You and Lily are so much younger, you're used to Miss or Mrs. And we're not in New York right now. With friends and colleagues, it's just Norma."

Ellen ducked her chin. "Thank you, Norma. I'm so excited to be working with you."

"Now," Norma deposited her purse on the foot of the bed, "where is that whiskey you promised?"

"Don't ask Alfred for that first," Tate warned with a grin.

~8~

By the next morning, the storm blew itself out, though the sky threatened to renew the assault, and the drifts were truly monumental.

Lynn awoke to the fragrance of Alfred's coffee wafting up from the kitchen. Grateful that he was always the earliest up, she slid out of bed and hurried through her morning rituals.

She and Alfred had a full bathroom tucked away through a dressing room lined in mirrors. Though they had help in the house in the summer, Lynn still often made up their bed herself. She pulled up the heavy blankets and, rather than tuck the soft feather pillows in the hard tube that turned them into a long bolster, she plumped the pillows and set them below the bed drape crowned with an open-winged golden swan. She admired the room, replete with swans and drapes, floral wallpaper and carpet, and decided that, busy as it was, she still loved it after so many years. Alfred's dresser was, as always, disciplined, with even his handkerchiefs stacked neatly next to the vials of medications and hair oil.

She scoured her closets in the dressing room, moving quickly in her choices of undergarments. "Trousers and heavy socks today," she murmured and shivered. She pulled on a wool sweater as well, and padded downstairs carrying her shoes, so as not to wake anyone else. All of the other bedroom doors remained shut fast.

Alfred met her at the kitchen door with a cup of coffee. He was already dressed in woolen trousers and an Irish sweater. She sighed in delight. "What have you conjured up for breakfast?"

"I put a baked omelet in the oven." Alfred bent down to check the status of the oven's contents. "And I'm making some toast points. I poured the juice too. Any movement from upstairs?"

The question was superfluous when they heard the soft voices of Tate and Norma coming their way. The two came into the kitchen through the swinging door to the dining room. Norma bowed to the weather and eschewed her usual fashion statement of floating gowns and bangle bracelets for the more mundane, and eminently more practical, full trousers and long velveteen jacket. Her additional touch of the usual scarves draped around her neck sufficed to maintain her standards. Tate was drab next to his mate. Tweed pants and muted plaid jacket, both in shades of a forest floor gasping for sunlight. Brown, tan, and a green so sickly as to be almost brown itself.

"We found our way!" Norma bubbled. "I hope it's all right we came right into the kitchen?"

"We don't stand on ceremony here at Ten Chimneys," Alfred assured them. "But we'll eat in the dining room. That table can accommodate all of us."

"Can we help?" Tate asked, accepting a cup of coffee from Alfred.

"Not a bit," Lynn said. "The kitchen is Alfred's domain, and if he doesn't ask for help, we are free and clear."

"Free, maybe," Alfred said, sending her a wink. "Clear, not hardly. I'll bring in the omelet, but you hired help can carry things in to the table."

"Hired?" Lynn snickered. She turned to Norma and Tate and whispered loud enough for Alfred to hear. "Those of us who live here subsist on only his kind words and an occasional nod. All others are paid by me." Alfred's frugality in domestic matters was well-known to his friends, but so was his generosity when warranted.

Lynn bundled a handful of flatware to Tate, and the tray of filled juice glasses to Norma, and held open the door to the dining room, hoping to stay out of the way of Norma's swaying scarves.

Downstairs in the laundry room, an outside door opened and closed, and laughter, accompanied by the sound of stomping feet, rose up the back stairs. Lynn went to the top of the stairs and called down, "Is that you, Harriet? Ed?"

"Unless you've hidden more people under the snow, of course it's us." Ed's booming voice grew louder as he and Harriet climbed up to the kitchen.

"We bring—" Harriet was cut off by Lynn's shriek.

"You bring a wave of icy cold air!" Lynn backed up into the kitchen. "Quick, Alfred! Coffee for these Arctic travelers."

"The cottage is not *that* far away," Alfred said

"Far enough to get chilled to the bone. And, looking at the clouds, it looks like we're in for more of that white stuff," Ed said. "Now, where's that coffee?"

"I'm sure you'll love it," Harriet said. She took a sip from the cup that Norma, back in the kitchen, handed her. "Ah! How ever do you do it, Alfred. It rivals Delmonico's."

"It's the egg, dear," Lynn said. "Cracked right into the grounds, shell and all. Then, he has some kind of abracadabra magic routine to cook it up."

"It is fabulous." Said, and echoed.

"I listened to the farm report on the radio this morning, and, you're right, Ed, there's more snow on the way. And high winds again," Alfred said.

"Not to change the subject," Lynn said, "much as I like the adulation for my husband's coffee and the weather report, but is there any movement from the girls upstairs?"

Norma shook her head. "Not yet. Not that we heard."

"Let's start without them. They need their beauty sleep," Lynn said.

Norma went into a dramatic pose. "They are the ingenues, here to learn at the feet of the Celestials." She indicated Alfred and Lynn before coming back to earth. "We can get some details going before they're needed for coaching and rehearsing."

"Perfect," Lynn said. "Let's eat."

Alfred got out a casserole holder for the omelet dish, while Lynn plucked toasts from the toaster, cut them into triangles, and set them on a plate. "The jams and honey are here, Norma. Can you carry them in? I think everything else is already on the table. Where's Tate?"

Tate came back into the kitchen. "Right here."

If Lynn were not looking at Harriet, she would have missed the faint indrawn breath, then the lips clamped tight and shoulders squared as if pulled up by marionette wires. Curious. Lynn turned to see if Alfred observed the same, but he was busy pulling the omelet out of the oven.

Led by Alfred and the egg dish, they adjourned to the dining room. Lynn, holding the door open, heard Harriet whisper to Ed as they passed, "He doesn't recognize me" and something about a blessing. *He?* Lynn thought. That could only mean Tate. There was no other *he*, other than Alfred, whom Harriet already met.

At the moment, Alfred was not available to consult. Lynn sighed and let the door swing shut behind her.

Alfred took his usual place with his back to the double doors, closed at the moment, leading into the flirtation room. Ed sat at his left and Harriet at his right. The other two moved into the next chairs, leaving two more open for "the girls," who could flank Lynn at the other end of the table, if they got there soon enough.

This was the maximum they liked to entertain, as far as Lynn was concerned, and she knew Alfred agreed with her. Eight was a nice intimate number. Any more guests, and one could not carry on a satisfactory conversation with any of them.

She looked around the table and felt warmed. She loved to entertain friends. Sprinkle in a new acquaintance or two and she was happy as a clam. She could relax and enjoy the company.

Harriet and Norma, next to each other, looked ready to go out on a shopping spree, hair and makeup in place, though they were far from anyone who cared. Even Lynn, the consummate fashion maven, looked more the country manor mistress than the elegant sophisticated Broadway actress she most certainly was.

Lynn stifled a chuckle when she swung her gaze to the men. Ed, half a head shorter than his wife, was a contrast in coloring. Where Harriet was fair, Ed was dark, his hair like a pomaded raven's wing, impeccable side-part in place. Lynn was secretly convinced that Ed was emulating Clark Gable, though, thank God, he didn't try for a matching moustache. He would look like a Chicago gangster.

Tate and Alfred resembled each other in height and style, though Lynn found Alfred the more attractive, of course. Tate was too blond for her taste, more like Van Johnson, who had upswept hair and deep blue eyes. Alfred's hair, while much thinner, was tamer, more disciplined than Tate's. Lynn didn't feel the need to run her fingers through her husband's hair. She much preferred running a finger up his leg... She had to stifle a giggle with one of Alfred's toast points. *Discipline, Lynnie*, she told herself.

"So," Tate turned to Ed, "is the weather out there as bad as it looks?"

"We had to shovel the snow away from the laundry room door before we could come in," Ed said. "Good thing you left the shovel out in the corner, Alfred."

"I cannot hear another word about the weather," Norma said, adding an eyeroll for emphasis. "I'm putting in a good word for the chef." She gave a little bow in Lynn's direction.

"Oh no, Norma," Alfred said. "I'm the chef, not Lynn. Her specialty is...what is it again, darling?"

"You know perfectly well the only thing I can make is English trifle." Lynn shook her butter knife at him. "And that only because it involves layers of cake that's already made. That, and fruit, of course."

"Well then." Norma turned to Alfred. "I applaud the man who married the woman who can make the trifle." They all joined Norma's applause.

"Alfred does the cooking and I do the praising," Lynn said. "We complement each other perfectly."

"Speaking of food," Ed said. "Is there enough to survive being snowed in?"

"Plenty," Alfred assured him. "Ben and his wife filled up the fridge before we arrived, and we butchered a pig last year, so there's plenty of pork, and more, in the freezer."

"Alfred canned so much garden produce we could probably feed the Royal Air Force," Lynn said.

"Don't worry. We hire help from the village for all that." Alfred dabbed his mouth with his napkin. "I love to garden, but I can do only so much by myself. Lynn cuts the flowers and I dig the weeds."

"Alfred always said he was simply a farmer who happens to act." Lynn smiled down the length of the table. That drew a chorus of incredulity. Everyone at the table knew—no, everyone in the world knew—that the team of Lunt and Fontanne were the premier acting couple on any stage.

"I hear the girls coming down," Ed said.

The double doors to the flirtation room opened and Ellen and Lily stepped in, talking and giggling.

"You two are certainly chipper today," Norma said, as she waved to the two empty chairs waiting for them.

"I slept like a log," Ellen said. "That little room at the end of the hall is just perfect for me. And plenty of closet space too."

"Were you both warm enough?" Lynn asked.

They both assured her they were cozy and comfortable. Once seated, they unfolded their napkins and accepted the offered plates of omelet Alfred sent down to them.

Lily tucked in to her eggs and toast, setting aside conversation for food and hot coffee.

Lynn, always eager to gather mannerisms and looks from anyone she met, set a close eye on Lily. She was not exactly a duplicate of Ellen, though both girls were young, both shapely, both rosy complexioned. Lily was the taller of the two. Where Ellen sported a cap of curls, Lily's hair, deep brown to match her eyes, was a waterfall that bubbled over her shoulders and cascaded down her back. So many actresses preferred to go blond, abandoning their dark hair to match some of the femme fatales of Hollywood. Lynn was glad to see that Lily was defying the blond craze. Blond would make her look like she was trying too hard. Of course, there were plenty of beauties with darker hair. Lynn was one of them. She was dedicated to retaining her dark hair, watching carefully when gray appeared. Someday, if Alfred were...no longer here, she might not watch so carefully. At that point, she would stop the onslaught.

When Lily Tremayne was mentioned to Lynn in New York as someone perfect for their new play, Lynn expected to find a girl pale and delicate. With a name like Lily, didn't that seem natural? But Lynn saw Lily had the bone structure to play roles that needed...a more substantial body.

-9-

Lily decided early on to escape her Midwest small town for New York. Her family was fine enough, what with a doting mother and a proud father. Even her two sisters were not a problem. Being the youngest, she had the advantage. The oldest was rather staid, even a stick-in-the-mud sometimes, refusing to join in the harmless fun of crawling out the window and hightailing it to the nearest party. Lily had to give her credit, though. Even though she was a rule follower extraordinaire, she never tattled on her youngest sister.

The middle sister, coming along only a year after that first baby, was totally oblivious to Lily, born six years after she was. Lily claimed that both her sisters seemed always to be facing the other way, wrapped up in their own friends, their own studies, their own selves. With the gap in years, Lily was pretty much left on her own. Rules were made for the first two, but she figured her parents were too tired by the time she came along, and the rules didn't seem to apply to her. She got away with murder.

Parties, drinking, fast driving—often in a "borrowed" car—her high school life was filled with excitement and secrets. Even though she was taller than most of her friends, including the boys, most of the time she faded into the trees, sometimes literally, when the going got too tough. In many ways, she was floundering. She didn't know what she wanted out of life. She couldn't seem to stop playing the bad girl. Well, at least the semi-bad girl.

So, she sometimes simply withdrew. She carved out a hideout in the woods. Nothing special, just a cleared area for a fire, an old canvas tent she rescued from the dump, a pile of firewood, and not much else.

In spite of no rules, or maybe because of no rules, she lived a life on the fringes of school, of friends, even of family. Much of it had to do with how she felt about boys. Or didn't feel. That proved to be more and more of a problem as she worked her way through high school. She couldn't admit to anyone, not anyone, that all the talk about good-looking guys, and making out, and petting, made her nervous. She felt all those things too. But toward girls, not boys.

In her town, in those early years, she expected to be stoned like the women in the Bible, if she broached that kind of subject.

She knew she had to leave. That much, she was sure of.

New York was that golden conglomeration in the East, where everybody could be what they were, and didn't have to pretend. Not just New York, but New York theater.

Another thing Lily knew. She loved being on stage. And she was good at it. Lily was in every school production. She could take on personas and live them out on stage, becoming someone everyone admired, or loved, or sometimes even hated. But that kind of hate was safe.

She auditioned, and got into, a couple of plays at the college in the next town over. Theater people, the college players and profs, were her kind of people. They had a love of life and the theater that matched, even surpassed, hers.

That year, the last college play of the spring season closed, and Lily was descending into mourning, as she usually did at the end of the season. "C'mon, Lily," Sal, one of the college girls, called from the wings. "We broke down the set, and we're the last ones left. Let's lock up and get out of here."

Lily went over to get their coats and grimaced at Sal. "Sure you can be seen with me in this sad ol' coat?" Yes, the coat was old, but Lily was apt to exaggerate when it came to the age or condition of her clothes. Tonight, she had on wide-legged Kate Hepburn trousers, paired with a form-fitting silk blouse that plunged in the front, stopped only by the last few mother-of-pearl buttons. Lily noticed Sal's eyes plunging with the silk.

"Absolutely. You can wear anything, anything at all." Sal was a year older, and she was gorgeous. Tall as Lily, but small-boned and graceful, like a ballet dancer. Lily loved just watching her walk. Somehow, tonight would be different. Watching Sal now, Lily could feel it.

Sal joined Lily and slid her hand across her shoulders. She whispered in Lily's ear, "I envy you your hair." She ran her hand up through Lily's hair.

Lily felt a frisson of pleasure run up her back. She turned her head to Sal, and Sal...kissed her. Though she never saw Sal again, that moment, and the ones that followed, sealed Lily to her future. New York. Theater. Living her true self.

•   •   •

New York was good to Lily. The going was a slog at times, but gradually, she built up experience. Tiny basement theaters, readings at bars, auditions with plenty of rejections. But enough work, even if it wasn't always theater work, to keep food on the table. Or on her lap, more likely, as she didn't have a table early on.

She ran into Mimi at an audition four years after moving to New York, when a director asked them to read a two-person scene. By some miracle, they both got the roles. It was a good off-off-Broadway production that, after a few nights, seemed to attract more critics, and even a handful of well-known actors.

That play paid well enough over its surprisingly long run that Mimi's and her relationship took on a new level of trust. They moved in together. Lily and Mimi played close to the vest, and few people, if any, knew they were lovers.

By scrimping and pooling earnings, they could afford a small studio, a fifth-floor walkup. The bathroom was miniscule, but at least, it wasn't a shared one down the hall. The second room doubled as living space, kitchen, bedroom, study, whatever needed to be done there. The sofa was a rollaway bed, and barely big enough for the both of them. But then, they didn't need much room in bed. Mimi was the best, and last, of Lily's lovers.

They rarely worked together, but they worked steadily. "When I left that wretched little town," Lily told Mimi, "I never dreamed I'd actually make it here. Most of all, I never thought I'd find the woman I'd commit to forever. You are…"

Mimi laughed. "I know I am." They were in bed, crushed against each other. Mimi raised herself up on one elbow and brushed a strand of hair from Lily's face. "I never would have made it if it weren't for you, Lily. You have stamina, and you pulled me through." She plopped back down. "Plus, it was love at first sight."

Lily learned to be her own best friend, never revealing too much. But with Mimi, she could open her heart and her mind. She knew Mimi felt the same. "For me too."

They tried to attend as much theater as time and budget allowed. On one particular afternoon, they attended a play getting powerful reviews. *She Knew Too Much* featured the main character of a gay woman. A gay woman who was clearly Mimi, even though the playwright named the character Millie.

Millie was Mimi's nickname as a child. It couldn't be coincidence. Lily knew about Mimi's tough past, knew Mimi's childhood nickname. It just could not be chance. It wasn't.

In the play, the character of Millie was not only gay, but a drunk, an addict, promiscuous and wicked. One of Millie's lovers committed suicide because of her. It was a devastating parallel to Mimi's earlier life. Gay, drugs and alcohol, slept with anybody and everybody, and nasty to almost everyone. The playwright knew all that, and used it. Lily also knew Mimi wasn't like that anymore. She made a clean break with that old life. But here it was again. The knowledge was bound to resurface.

Mimi sat stiff in her seat, hands gripping the armrests.

"Let's go," Lily said, as the lights came up for intermission.

"No! I'm sticking it out to the end," Mimi whispered. "Let's see if they got all the dirty details in."

Lily could only take hold of Mimi's hand and tough it out.

Once home, Lily slammed the door, and set out pacing. "Why are they doing this to you?"

"To *us!*" Mimi broke in. "Because of me, they pulled you right in too. People *know* that...all the...the old life...is long gone, why are they dredging it up now?"

Because someone thinks it makes a good story that'll make a ton of money. But Lily didn't say it.

Mimi was white as a sheet. She clenched and unclenched her hands, and her head shook back and forth like a metronome. "I can't let them do this! People don't know me that way anymore. I changed. I changed everything about me...after that."

"No one's going to hate you, Mimi. They all know the real you." Lily sat down beside her and drew her into an embrace. "We'll be okay."

"No. No, we won't," Mimi cried. "I'll end up getting cut off from everybody!" She turned to Lily. "I'll never work again."

"Everybody knows it's only theater. Anybody that's important, that is. The others don't count anyway."

"I'll die!" Her tears soaked Lily's shoulder. "I can't live this down. The suicide of Millie's friend at the end—"

"Sh-h-h! We'll get through this together."

Lily spent the night consoling and cajoling, but it didn't seem to lessen the trauma. Mimi removed herself more and more as the night went on, until, by dawn, she was frigid and totally withdrawn.

When they gathered themselves the next day and left for their jobs, Lily was frantic with worry. But she couldn't figure out what to do, beyond trying to carry on as normal, a sign to Mimi that all would still be...normal. It was all too cloudy, too confusing. The two went their separate ways with a hand squeeze and tight looks, which gave nothing away.

After her last performance of that evening, Mimi hanged herself in the fly tower above the stage.

She Knew Too Much closed a year later, without fanfare. Lily was not in town to see it.

For a little while, Lily worked in a fog. Life felt so very empty. But she had to eat, and she realized she couldn't stay in New York. Within a few months, an opportunity arose with a repertory company in Boston, and she jumped at the chance to leave the pain behind.

Of course, the pain moved with her.

So, she drove herself hard, arriving at the theater early, leaving late. Anything to purge the hollow part in her heart. She took parts that required more of her, always bettering herself. Two years and the hurt subsided to a dull sheen.

She was getting noticed. Critics praised her intensity, though added that she sometimes went over the top. One director finally told her he was recommending her for a role in Alfred Lunt's and Lynn Fontanne's new play in New York. A thrumming grew in her, and she recognized it as a remnant of the old excitement, the lure that drew her to New York in the first place. Perhaps she could recover some of the joy she lost. It was worth a try.

-10-

For Alfred, breakfast at the estate was never taken lightly. He loved to cook, and Lynn knew that with company in the house, he was in his element. "Stoking the furnace," he called the morning meal. And with a long day of work ahead of them, they would need the energy.

Lynn buttered her toast and looked around the table. Her gaze lighted on Ellen. Ellen Lang looked a lot like Shirley Temple when she was a child. The hair, at least. Light hair, without being truly blond, full of curls, as if trying to explode from her head. Bright green eyes looked intelligent and curious. Round cheeks flanked a little rosebud mouth that smiled a lot. Sweetness personified. Lynn hoped that wouldn't hold her back from heavier roles. Time would tell.

These two young ladies, Ellen and Lily both, seemed comfortable with themselves, as Lynn herself was. Lynn's beauty, as everyone commented on, was of the more mature type, though everyone told her she looked years younger than her age. She was pleased with the compliments, but she never succumbed to them. She simply understood how to take care of herself. All of her photos showed that. No double chin, no wrinkles, flawless complexion, shining hair pulled back into a soft chignon at the nape of her neck, expressive gestures with those long beautifully refined hands. No need for further embellishments. Perhaps a strand of pearls when the occasion called for it, but nothing more. More, even earrings, would go beyond the simplicity she preferred.

Lynn perused the two girls whom she and Alfred took under their wings. They looked to have potential for high success on the stage. They possessed the looks and the presence to make something of themselves. Though right now, at breakfast in small-town Wisconsin, they didn't shine much. Hair was combed, to be sure, but still in a bit of disarray. No fancy dress here. Only trousers–most welcome in the winter, even if the house was warm–and a layer of tops under a heavy tunic for Lily, with a deep burgundy cowl-collared sweater under a stylish blazer for Ellen.

No haute couture, but Lynn was satisfied that both girls chose practicality over fashion, as did all the women in the room. No bare legs today, nor legs meagerly protected by silk stockings. She shivered, revealing her British dread of cold. Time to think of something else.

She shifted to considering the girls' real value–their talents and drives. Lynn was more than satisfied at the coup of hiring them both while they were still open to developing new directions, and could be taught and molded. Of course, Alfred felt—and she herself did as well—that anyone working with them must be willing to be taught and molded. The Lunts had a grand reputation of "making" actors, especially the willing ones.

She realized Alfred was talking to her. "Sorry, darling. What were you saying?"

"Whenever we're ready, we can move to the drawing room," Alfred said. "There's plenty of room. I've lit a small fire."

There was general agreement around the table.

"Alfred, slow down." Lynn turned to the others. "Please don't rush. We've plenty of time. Once we start, we tend to lose track of everything, don't we, darling?" She toasted Alfred with a glass of orange juice. "Isn't it wonderful that we can get oranges, even in the middle of winter? One would think we're back in New York."

Norma exploded with a deep guffaw, a bit unseemly for such a doyenne. But she appeared unconcerned with the outburst. She fluffed the scarf draped around her neck. "New York has streetlights *and* oranges, even in the middle of winter."

"It is plenty dark around here," Harriet said. "But it's also peaceful. I love it."

"That's why Alfred and I insist on spending our summers here in Wisconsin," Lynn said. "It's a real refuge. You must return when the weather is warm and sunny. We can get outside and use the pool."

"Invitation accepted," Ed said, punctuating his words by stabbing the air with his fork.

Lynn nibbled on her last toast point, and settled back to enjoy the company and conversation before they set off to work. They certainly were a diverse crowd. Norma, the elder stateswoman of the theater, was carrying on a tete-a-tete with Harriet, apparently oblivious to the other woman's scars. If not oblivious, then charitable at feigning unconcern. *If that's the case,* Lynn thought, *she is the consummate actress, and we are lucky to have her.*

Lily jabbed at her eggs and toast as if she had not eaten for a week. No conversation there, at the moment. She was still pretty much an unknown to Lynn, having only secured this invitation because of their theater company's recommendation. That, and a request to take her in for the kind of fine-tuned training the Lunts were known for.

Ellen was another story. Her plea for help at a spontaneous backstage visit, showed gumption, and Lynn was appreciative of gumption. While Ellen was clearly enjoying Alfred's omelet, her gaze was ever-moving, scanning the other guests and listening with an intent look on her face. Lynn smiled. *She should be an eager student. It looks like she will soak up everything we can give her.*

Ed and Alfred were leaning close, apparently discussing the play and its rewrites with some intensity. Though Lynn couldn't hear what they were saying, she watched both men exchange frowns, then quizzical looks, then hearty laughs, before they stood up in unison and, still talking, carried their dishes to the kitchen.

"Guess that's the signal," Tate said, rising and stacking his dishes before heading into the kitchen too.

Norma and Harriet looked up, apparently surprised by the sudden dearth of men. "I think we're being left behind," Norma said. "Maybe we should stall and see if they'll start washing dishes."

Lynn laughed, knowing how meticulous Alfred was concerning his kitchen. "I'm not going to let that happen." She stood and picked up her dishes. "Not if I have anything to say about it. We can do dishes after dinner tonight. Based on how involved he and Ed are, I know how Alfred will react if he can't get to his beloved script. Let's get the table cleared, at least, and then we can get to work."

Ellen was up immediately, but Lily said, "I'll be there in a minute. I want to finish this." She brandished a toast point and a glass of orange juice.

"Darling, don't make Alfred wait." Lynn's voice held a gentle warning, just as Ed and Alfred came through from the kitchen, still talking, and disappeared into the flirtation room on the way to the drawing room.

-11-

When Lynn opened the door to the drawing room, and stepped in, Ellen, right behind her, gave a gasp and stopped dead. The others piled up behind her, craning to look around her or over her shoulder.

Lynn, accustomed to the effect of the room on others, took stock with fresh eyes. Yes, it was a splendid room.

Just inside the door to the left was a grand piano. But not just any piano. Painted white, and embellished with fanciful flourishes and Chinoiserie figures, the cover stood open, revealing a bright red background on which was painted Orpheus charming the wild animals. Behind the piano, a small table held a Scrabble box, waiting for someone to play.

Along the wall, an ample fireplace, where a cheery fire was already mumbling and whistling, fronted by two pairs of coral chairs, plush, and carved in full Victorian extravaganza. Beyond, another gaming table with a couple of decks of cards. Opposite the fireplace, a blue velvet settee beckoned. Three could sit in a cozy triad, or one person could nap, curled up a bit.

"I can't believe this!" Ellen said. "Look at the wall murals! They're gorgeous, Miss Fontanne." She finally released the others by walking into the room, then spinning slowly to take it all in. Murals of Old Testament drama, done in soft pastels, punctuated the areas between windows. The ceiling was embellished with clouds and cherubs.

"We had a stage designer out," Alfred said. "Turned out pretty lovely, wouldn't you say?"

Lynn realized that many would find the furniture and décor rather odd. Nothing really matched. But whenever she and Alfred found something they liked, they bought it. It didn't matter if Victorian sat side by side with Chinese, or Empire with Louis XIV. Dramatic and fun, those were the watchwords. That, and comfortable, of course. Lynn forced herself out of reverie. "Perhaps we should get started, if that's all right with everyone."

Murmurs of assent. The group split and settled on the various pieces of furniture.

Ed handed out new pages for the play. "I managed to get copies of the early rewrites made before we left the city. But keep your pencils handy. I'm sure there are going to be more."

Tate excused himself to go upstairs and finish unpacking, considering he wasn't part of the theater ensemble. They waved him goodbye.

The morning settled into a leisurely routine. People shifted from chair to settee to piano bench, or wandered around the room. Once in a while, Lily or Ellen went out to the flirtation room window to check the weather. For a while, it looked like an old silent film, with actors mouthing lines and trying out stances. Faces went from shocked to sad to elated and back again.

Finally, like birds homing in on a nest, they settled in place and began an informal run-through of new scenes. By the time lunch would roll around, they hoped to try out many of Ed's rewrites. Alfred warned them not to voice concerns or kudos, but to mark spots they felt were rough, out of sync, or especially resonant. They could share notes after lunch.

In the meantime, Lynn shared whispered suggestions with Alfred, who seemed to be jotting notes and drawing circles at a rather fast pace.

The morning sped onward.

•   •   •

The afternoon almost mirrored the morning, though Tate became a silent audience, plunking down on a chair in the corner, alternately reading and looking up to listen to the actors running their lines.

Sometimes the lines didn't reflect the romantic comedic tone of the piece, even the rewrites falling flat. Then, the tone turned more serious as they discussed Ed's revisions, and Alfred's and Lynn's suggestions. Neither Lily nor Ellen said anything, which pleased Lynn. They were supporting roles to start with, and, at this point, should have little say in the direction of the action. Alfred, as usual, filled the void. He always had plenty of ideas, most of which enhanced everyone's roles, as well as the arc of the action. Lynn, herself an astute judge, did not hesitate to disagree with him, but learned early on how to wield a strong hand in a velvet glove.

But they both could be firm taskmasters, playing and replaying a scene multiple times.

"Here, Ellen," Lynn said. "Come over here." She led Ellen to the fireplace and turned her back to the fire. "Try those lines here. Standing sometimes helps clarify what you're saying."

But it didn't quite work there either. "Turn this way." "Set one foot a bit forward." "Slip your hand in your pocket. No, not that far. Just halfway down your fingertips." "Hmm. Now shove your hand all the way down." "Frown." "Not so much." And on and on into the afternoon.

It wasn't only Ellen taking the brunt of direction. "Lily, you're in this scene with Ellen. Read that entire page. Stop when you feel—"

Lynn clenched a hand and held it up. "When you feel the action peaking."

Then it was, "Lean into her," and "Not so fast. Feel the natural pauses." "Try shaking a finger...no, that's too much. Don't push the drama."

"This is a dance, ladies. Don't turn it into a fencing match." That last from Alfred.

Lynn retreated to share the settee with Harriet, observing the action from the sidelines. Harriet tucked her feet under her and leaned against the armrest. Lynn watched her friend growing more and more limp as she relaxed against the cushions. Too much excitement and a long train journey.

Finally, Harriet's eyes fluttered and she appeared to be drifting asleep. Then, she would twitch awake, reposition herself, and begin the process all over again.

In one of Harriet's quiet periods, Lynn slid away. She walked over to Norma who was following everything from a chair in front of the fireplace. Lynn lowered herself into a matching chair and set her elbow on the arm, chin in hand. "The girls will be fine, don't you think? They seem to take direction well."

Norma put her finger on the lines Ellen was delivering. Over and over, the same few lines, Ellen went forward and back, while Alfred adjusted her voice, her stance, the tilt of her head. On and on.

"Ellen truly listens," Norma said. "On the other hand, Lily seems pretty headstrong." She waved her hand at Lily, who was sitting on the piano bench, script open on her lap, reading her lines to herself. "She frowns more than she smiles. I don't think she's happy."

"Maybe not," Lynn said.

Norma shrugged. "She'll be fine. She takes direction well most of the time. What about Ellen? She's younger, I think. At least, she acts younger. Bright and...flighty? No, maybe that's not right." She adjusted the blue sweater she added to her ensemble after lunch, pulling the shawl collar up to nestle around her ears. In addition, she swept a scarf around her neck to secure the collar more firmly.

Lynn, already garbed in the warmest trousers she owned, silently thanked Hepburn for setting that particular style, at least for home wear. "Ellen felt so genuine, so eager, when we saw her in New York, we decided to take a chance." Lynn shrugged. "Time will tell. I'll just work harder with her. It appears that Alfred has both of them well in hand."

"I love working with Alfred," Norma said. "He is tough, there's no doubt about that, but he's kind and generous to a fault. He makes me a better actress."

Lynn laughed. "You've been acting longer than we have, Norma. You already were a terrific actress when we met you. But thank you, on Alfred's behalf. I shall pass along the compliment."

"Lynnie, come on over here," Alfred called. "Let's run this whole scene with Ellen. See how the rewrites work. I may have some ideas."

Lynn whispered to Norma, "He *always* has ideas. I hope these are as good as they usually are." She showed Norma crossed fingers, rose in a fluid motion, and swept over to Alfred.

~12~

Ellen was a born actress. At least, that's what her mother told her. Ellen and her sister both. When Ellen's father died, he left his family well-taken care of. But that didn't mean they were over-the-top wealthy, not like the people living along Lake Michigan on Chicago's Gold Coast. They were much farther inland.

Their mother began taking her girls to photo shoots for catalogs and magazines where children were needed. They were adorable, and had little trouble getting hired. Both of them had the wild curls so popular on children, thanks to Shirley Temple. They weren't twins, but made an attractive pair, Amelia open and laughing with eyes all a-glitter, Ellen looking out from under long fringes of eyelashes and smiling with that little rosebud mouth. They only got cuter as they got older.

"The Triumvirate," Mother called the three of them. Always together, always professional. Sometimes they auditioned for parts on the stage as well, and that gave both girls a thirst for theater that matched their mother's. They could take the 'L' downtown to see everything from musicals to Shakespeare, old favorites to avant-garde pieces. The Triumvirate was in heaven.

More than Ellen, her sister was the one who loved acting, and, at that point, Mother shepherded them in that direction. The modeling was left by the wayside.

Amelia loved taking on new personas, people she would never dream of being in real life. Ellen was a bit more shy about starting to trumpet lines in public. She was convinced that people would equate a role with the real person playing it. Her friends always seemed to do that with the movie stars they fawned over. Fred Astaire certainly danced his way down the grocery aisles, Cary Grant was always funny, Judy Garland looked at everything wide-eyed, Myrna Loy was a femme fatale in real life. Ellen didn't want that happening to her.

Her mother and her sister kept encouraging. "You love theater so, and you keep spouting lines from things we've seen. You remember everything," her mother said. "Why don't you audition?"

"Oh, I wouldn't dare!" Ellen said.

"For heaven's sake, Ellen," Amelia said, "you're a big girl now. Almost in high school already. Get involved!"

Ellen could almost hear the wheels turning in her head. She had been in front of a camera for still shots often enough. Maybe... "I'll do it, if you'll do it. Together." To say it out loud to her sister surprised even Ellen herself.

Amelia, stunned into silence for a moment, stuck her hand out. "It's a deal."

Well, now I have *to do it!* Ellen thought. She loved her sister dearly, and knew it would break Amelia's heart if Ellen didn't follow through. She took a deep breath and clutched her sister's hand. "It's a deal."

Two of the Triumvirate were off and running. They took small roles in small theaters, and tried to perform in the same plays, which didn't always work, of course, but they tried. Ellen always stuck to the one-line roles, while Amelia charged forward.

Finally, Amelia issued a challenge after high school one day. "Ellen, Goodman Theater put out a call. There's a little comedy slated for right before Christmas, and I signed both of us up."

Ellen blanched. "You can't mean..." The Goodman was theater heaven for her.

"Yes, I can! We can play two sisters." She grabbed Ellen by the shoulders. "And it's going to be fun!"

Ellen just wanted to escape. She dashed to the girls' bathroom. "The Goodman! Not the Goodman," she whispered. She repeated it, like a mantra. Looking in the mirror, she saw a terrified girl—eyebrows as high as the sky, eyes with dilated pupils, hair awry. She leaned in, watching her chin begin to tremble.

Amelia strode in and whirled her around. "We are going to do this." She looked Ellen in the eye. "And we are going to be wonderful. I guarantee it."

Amelia never let Ellen down before. Ellen heard a tiny voice in her head say, "She's right, you know. If she's there, you can do it." It didn't help to put her hands over her ears.

"Time to knock 'em dead!" Amelia said. "C'mon. Let's get to that audition."

Maybe we won't make it. Ellen tried to convince herself, but that little voice reared its head again. "You'll make it. And you'll be good." *Oh, God, what am I getting myself into?*

They did make it. But the best surprise was, they were good. The roles seemed made for them. Two sisters, at odds at first, then working through their differences to come to appreciate one another. It was a small subplot in a large company, but it added some comedic spice to the ensemble.

On closing night, they fell into each other's arms, laughing. "We did it!" Ellen sang.

"*You* did it," Amelia said. "I did this for you, and you did it! And you can get even better."

A prophecy that came true. But not for both of them.

Amelia got larger and larger roles, but as that happened, she got involved with the wilder crowds. Alcohol, morphine, cocaine, heroin. Sex with anyone. Amelia went down a very deep rabbit hole, very, very fast.

Ellen was powerless to help her. Their mother tried everything, from pleadings to promises. Nothing worked. When she threatened to send Amelia to the Narco Farm in Lexington, Kentucky, for treatment and incarceration, Amelia rebelled.

She ran away. She not only ran away, she disappeared.

From that moment on, Ellen's mother declined in health. After Ellen graduated from high school, she stayed in Chicago to care for her ailing mother, and continue acting. But as with her sister, Ellen was powerless to heal her mother's broken body, much less her soul. For almost three years, her mother hung on, ultimately falling into a delirium just before she died.

As if in mockery, two days after her mother died and was buried, Ellen received a postcard. "Don't worry. I'm fine. Your loving Sis." The postmark was blurred, but not so much that Ellen couldn't discern "New York City" through the smudged ink. No return address. Nothing but that succinct handwritten note.

It took very little time to sell the Chicago house, and she stayed with a friend until her mother's estate was settled. Then, armed with letters of recommendation, a purse containing money and proof of funds transferred, Ellen got on a train headed for New York City. With her was a valise and a suitcase stuffed with all of her earthly goods. She would first find work. Wires sent out from Chicago theater impresarios brought responses that were favorable. Act, yes. But most important, maybe she could find her sister.

-13-

The winter sun was drifting down in Wisconsin. The afternoon light waned as the group worked. Tate drifted in and out of the drawing room, ignored by Lynn and the rest of the company. Snow continued to fall, silent into the dark.

Dinner was an informal congenial affair, with everyone creating their own sandwiches in the kitchen, grabbing raw carrot sticks and other vegetables, and adjourning to the dining room, where conversation continued to flow.

"Theater, theater, theater! Is that all you people talk about?" Tate smiled as he said it. "I should've stayed in New York."

Norma patted him on the arm. "You know you would never get enough done there. I'd come home and you'd complain about being lonely and not accomplishing enough."

Tate leaned over to bestow a quick kiss on her cheek. "I know, love, I know. After dinner, I'll bring down my briefcase and secrete myself in the... Where shall I closet myself, Lynn?"

"The library will be perfect," Lynn said. "I'll bring in a fur throw for you, and we'll build a fire in there too. You can spread out on the desk. Although it's not terribly large. Maybe the couch would work too."

"Just don't sink into the overstuffed chair," Alfred said. "I have it on good authority, that particular chair is better than a sleeping pill."

"Your 'good authority' is yourself, darling." Lynn sent him a smirk. "I've seen you slumbering in that chair more than once."

"As I said, Tate, avoid that chair."

"Where's the wine, Alfred?" Ed asked. "Something to wash down the repast."

Alfred shook his head. "We'll save the wine for another dinner."

Ed shrugged, but frowned. "Ah, well. Something to look forward to."

"But brandy in the drawing room when we've finished here," Lynn said. "Or something else if you wish. We also have sherry, if I'm not mistaken, yes, Alfred?"

"Either one," Alfred agreed. "A little something to warm you up before bed."

Ed waved his fork toward the window. "Considering I have to go out in that stuff, can't wait."

Dinner over, they cleared the table, cleaned the kitchen, leaving the dishes to drain and air dry. Lynn and Alfred shooed them back to the drawing room, while the two of them finished up a few things in the kitchen.

"Harriet looks tired," Lynn said, when she was alone with Alfred. "She fell asleep several times earlier, though I don't think anyone else noticed. She's been run ragged, what with typing lines for Ed, and fielding dialogue for him."

Alfred put a decanter of brandy and a bottle of whiskey on a silver tray, lining the perimeter with highball glasses with ice, and brandy snifters. "She is a real workhorse. I don't think people realize how much effort she puts into things. She's always got something going. Like a perpetual motion machine."

Lynn grabbed a stack of cocktail napkins and motioned Alfred out the door. "Put the tray on the table by the piano, Alfred. It'll be out of the way there."

Alfred snorted. "As long as Ed doesn't spot it. He's got quite a nose for the booze."

"We'll keep him too busy to notice it," Lynn said, as they descended the steps into the drawing room.

Tate followed them in, briefcase and booklets in hand. "I should be able to get a lot done tonight," he said, "considering how late you theater people manage to stay awake."

"Oh, you don't have to stay up as late as we do," Norma said. "It must seem like we go on forever, once we get started."

"Which means we may get to bed quite late," Lynn said. "Let's make breakfast an informal affair. Alfred can cook when he's ready, and everyone can come into the dining room whenever they get up. We won't set a time or wait for everybody to appear. How is that?"

Everyone decided that would be quite agreeable.

Lynn directed Alfred to set his tray of liquor on the table, and she added her cocktail napkins to the collection. "Come on, Tate. I'll show you the library," she said. She took his elbow and steered him to a flight of four steps leading off the drawing room. "Up here."

He trailed her up the steps. "Is that the infamous sleeping chair?" He gestured toward the plump yellow brocade chair next to the fireplace. "Sure looks comfortable enough to swallow up a tired person. I hope I won't sink out of sight."

They shared a chuckle. "No," Lynn said, "it's Alfred's favorite, and, as much as he denies it, he does drift off occasionally." She shifted to a whisper. "But then, so do I. I don't dare sit down with a script or I'd never finish. But now you've been warned. *Cave sellam!* Beware the chair!"

Tate looked around, nodding. "Perfectly satisfactory. Still a bit chilly in here, though. Should I light the fire?"

"That would be grand. Thank you," Lynn said. "It seems Alfred was taking care of the drinks and didn't get to it." She gestured to the desk. "Put your work down, and I'll show you the loo." She opened a door and stepped through into a short hallway. "Let me grab that fur throw." She opened the door to the yellow room, went in, and swept up a throw off the chaise longue. "This is really the coldest room in the house, even in the summer." She shut the door behind her. "But here's the toilet." She opened another door nearby and left it ajar. "Much better than having to run all the way upstairs."

"How on earth do you ever find your way around this house? It's like a maze!" Tate stood with his mouth open.

"It's not that difficult, once you've been here," Lynn said. "You can exit the library into the drawing room, just as we came in. Or you can go this back way, past the toilet, and come out in the flirtation room. That way you don't have to listen to our cacklings in the drawing room. You can bypass us entirely."

"Ingenious," Tate said. "Well, then I won't bother you by breaking in to say goodnight. I'll just come down and say it now."

They both moved back into the drawing room, where Tate made the rounds of goodnights, and retreated to the library, closing the door behind him.

"Wait!" Alfred went to the library door, brandy snifter in hand. The door opened again, showing Tate with a quizzical look on his face. Until he saw Alfred's offering.

"Oh, you are a good man, Alfred," Tate said, taking the proffered brandy snifter.

"Always ready to please," Alfred answered, bowing. "This will warm you up whenever you need it. And so, I bid you goodnight."

Tate returned the bow, saluted with the snifter, and closed the door to the library.

"How about tickling the ol' ivories, Alfred?" Ed asked. "Or are the piano keys too dusty?"

"Edward!" Harriet's comment was an unadulterated chide.

Ed held up his hands in surrender. "Just thought we could get some music started."

Lynn came to the rescue. "Oh, we don't play. But a lot of our friends from New York do. So, we had the piano sent out from New York." She shrugged. "Sorry, no music tonight, although the piano does get used on occasion."

Norma stepped up. "I have some questions about delivery in a couple of spots." Attention swiveled to the play and their roles, saving Ed–or rather, Harriet– any embarrassment.

Alfred turned to the rest, spread his arms, and said, "Very good. Let's get started. The night is young."

~14~

Harriet took up her position on the settee and opened Ed's script. "Tell me when you want me to mark something, Ed." She pulled a pencil from atop her ear.

"You can be sure I will," Ed said. He settled in one of the chairs before the fireplace. "I'll be listening for rough spots, so pay attention."

Lynn gave Alfred one of her "don't go there" looks, hoping to forestall any major blowups. She knew Alfred could contain himself, but she wasn't so sure about Ed. This was the first time they worked with him, and based on his irascible mood on the trip out, this collaboration could be thorny. Although, maybe he was just tired from the trip.

They worked with Ellen and Lily first, honing one scene Ed rewrote, then moving on to another that included Norma. With Norma involved, neither Alfred nor Ed interrupted them until the scene was complete. Then everyone talked at once, praising Norma for holding the tone steady when the girls started to wander into melodrama.

"Harriet!" Ed's voice cut through the celebration. "You're supposed to—"

Lynn cut him off before his angry tone of voice could slice into his wife. "Harriet, dear, you look exhausted. We've been working you to the bone. Why don't you head off to bed?" She walked to the window. "It's starting to snow again, and the wind is picking up. Better to go up to the cottage now, before it gets worse."

Harriet sent Lynn a look of unfettered gratitude. A relaxation of the muscles around her eyes, a brief opening of her mouth, a lowering of her shoulders. Lynn noted it all. Movements that could be incorporated into a future role, perhaps. Always on the lookout for improvement.

"Don't worry about me, Ed," Harriet said. "I know you probably want to stay and work a bit longer. I'll bundle up and head for bed. Everything should be nice and warm by the time you come up."

"Turn the porch light on," Ed said. "And make sure you don't turn it off when you go to bed. Don't make me get lost in the snow."

Harriet nodded and handed off her script to Ed. She waved a quick goodnight to everyone and left the drawing room. Lynn heard her go down the main staircase. Shortly after, an outer door opened, then closed.

Perhaps we should make sure she gets to the cottage, Lynn thought after a few short minutes. "Lily, look out the flirtation room window and see if you can see Harriet."

Lily popped up from the piano bench and went to look. "I can't see a thing," she called. "Too much snow blowing around. It's dark as sin out there." Lynn could see her peering into the night. "Oh, wait! I think I saw the porch light go on." She came back down into the drawing room.

"Close the door, dear. Let's keep the heat in," Lynn said. "Are you sure you saw the light on?"

"The wind dropped for a minute, and I saw a glow where the porch should be," Lily said. "I think she turned a light on inside too. It's pretty hard to see out there."

"Then I'd better get these changes finished before I leave," Ed said. "I'll be in the kitchen. I'll say goodnight now, and leave from there when I'm done." He gathered up his papers and headed out of the drawing room.

Lynn turned to Ellen and pointed to a passage to read aloud. Meanwhile, Norma and Alfred helped Lily with the rapid back and forth required in another scene. The room was large enough, and the scenes without dramatic speeches, that they could work at opposite ends and not disturb each other.

At one point, Lily headed for the piano, clearly about to use it as a place to prop herself in a melodramatic pose. Lynn and Alfred exchanged a glance and a smirk when Lily realized Alfred positioned a small Chinoiserie table just so no one could lean on his elaborately painted piano. No chance to scratch the paint or smudge the patina.

Lynn turned back to Ellen and had her repeat the scene.

After many read-throughs, Ellen began yawning, hiding most yawns behind a hand or her script. "If you don't need me anymore, I'd really like to go up to bed. I think watching Harriet nod off got me started too."

"We've worked you back and forth, haven't we?" Alfred said, halting Lily mid-speech. "Why don't you head on up, Ellen?"

Ellen sighed and rolled up her script. "I'll take this with me. Maybe I can stay awake long enough to read through it a couple more times. I really appreciated the help, Miss Fontanne, Mr. Lunt." She slipped out, closing the door behind her.

Footfalls went up the steps, a toilet flushed upstairs, a door closed with a bang, and all was quiet.

Having seated herself, Lily, now hunched over on the piano bench, murmured lines *sotto voce*. Her hands fluttered here and there, and she appeared to be trying out different facial expressions as well. Lynn watched her with satisfaction. At last, the girl seemed to be taking direction seriously. She turned her attention to Norma and Alfred, now huddled on the settee.

Lynn pulled a chair over to the little table in front of Alfred and Norma. She set her script down and picked up a pencil. "Change this. Maybe move this way here." She licked her lips as she underlined, ticked, added marginalia. Back and forth, the three of them talked over fine points.

Lily abandoned her piano bench to go to the flirtation room and apparently check on the storm. She came back in an unusual hurry.

Lynn wondered why the rush. "What is it, dear?" Lynn asked, trying for subtlety.

"I'm *so* cold," Lily said, wiping a hand across her eyes. "I think the weather is taking its toll."

"Maybe you should head for bed too," Alfred said. "We wouldn't want you to get sick."

"What I really need is a hot bath," Lily said.

"Go ahead," Lynn said, but Lily was on her way out.

Soon, the bedroom door at the top of the stairs closed with a thud.

"Are we good for maybe another hour?" Lynn asked. They reached an important spot in the scene they were discussing, and she hated to quit just then. "Or even another half-hour?"

"Darling, you know I could go on all night," Alfred said, reaching over to give her hand a squeeze.

"Not all night, Alfred, please." Norma laughed. "I am no longer a spring chicken. I need my beauty sleep." She patted her hair with an exaggerated gesture. "But I can concede a half-hour, if you must."

They set to work again.

A half-hour wasn't long enough to complete what they wanted to, and they were getting close to the hour mark when they were interrupted.

Ed came through the doors to the drawing room.

"I thought you were gone already," Norma said.

"I finished the re-writes, so I would be," Ed said, "but I can't find my coat."

"What do you mean, you can't find your coat?" Alfred said. "It's on the rack in the laundry room."

"No, it's not." Ed's irritation was crystal clear in the tone of his voice. "There are others there, but not mine. What did you do with it?"

Alfred closed his script on a pencil to mark his spot. "Come on. I'll go down with you. It's got to be there somewhere. I hung it up myself." He stood up, gave Lynn a quick peck on the cheek and excused himself.

The two men left, Ed grumbling, Alfred shaking his head.

"They'll find it," Lynn said. "Alfred is nothing if not meticulous."

"Knowing Ed," Norma said, "he probably threw it on the floor and kicked it into a corner."

They were still laughing over various scenarios about the missing coat when Alfred reappeared.

"I have no idea what happened to it," Alfred said, "but Ed was right. It wasn't there. I even checked in the foyer closet, thinking maybe someone moved it."

Lynn pursed her lips. "We didn't even use the foyer, and certainly not the closet, but it was worth a peek anyway."

Alfred said, "We couldn't find his coat anywhere. Harriet's coat is gone, of course. Tate's is there, but not Ed's." He dropped down onto the settee next to Lynn. "We'll look again tomorrow. It has to be somewhere. Maybe someone took it up to a bedroom."

"The girls are in bed. We're not going to disturb them now," Lynn said. "It's far too late, and they're sleeping, I'm sure."

Norma nodded. "Alfred's right. It's probably upstairs somewhere. Tomorrow's soon enough." She sat up, her head tilted to one side. "So, where's Ed now?"

"He headed up to the cottage. I lent him one of my coats," Alfred said. "His galoshes and hat were still there, though. He looked like a Russian bear, my coat's so long on him."

Lynn giggled. "I can imagine. He's a lot shorter than most men."

"Will he be all right?" Norma asked. "Maybe you should watch him out the window."

Alfred leaped up and headed for the flirtation room. "Good idea. The wind dropped, so he should be able to find his way." Within a few minutes, he was back. "I think I could see his bulk through the snow. But I waited until I saw the porch light go off."

"Then he made it," Lynn said. She stood up and dropped her script on the table. "I think it's time we went to bed. What time is it?"

Norma checked her wristwatch. "Almost three." She shook herself. "It's a good time to stop. I'm off to bed."

"What about Tate?" Lynn stood at the bottom of the steps leading to the library. "There's still a light on in there. I can see it through the crack under the door."

"Oh, don't worry about Tate," Norma said. "When he's working late at home, he often spends the night in the study. He just gets so involved, he loses track of time. We finally moved a sofa in, so he could stretch out in comfort. He always says he doesn't want to disturb me by rummaging around and coming to bed after I'm asleep." She put a finger to her lips. "Truth be told, I don't mind at all."

Lynn said, "There's a couch in the library here too."

"If he didn't fall asleep in the chair already," Alfred said.

"Like you do, darling." Lynn smiled. She took Norma's hand, and led her out of the drawing room. "Bank the fire and turn off the lights, please, Alfred."

"I'll be right up," Alfred said, poker in his hand, "as soon as I get the firescreen in place."

-15-

The next day dawned bright, with only wisps of clouds scudding across the sun, tossing skeletal shadows from the trees swaying in the considerable wind.

Alfred was making blueberry pancakes, and Lynn was filling a pitcher with apple juice, when the outside door downstairs in the laundry room opened, then closed with a firm thud. Ed's and Harriet's voices came up to the kitchen. Complaining, based on the tone.

Lynn went to the back stairs and called down, "Shake off the snow and come on up. Alfred's got the coffee brewing."

They appeared, Harriet clutching a small train case, both of them in wool trousers and argyle-patterned sweaters. "Ed insisted we get down here before lunch. So, pardon my lack of makeup. I brought it down with me, so I can get my face on after breakfast."

"Brunch," Alfred said. "It's really too late to call it breakfast. I made a proper brunch."

"We were just about to go through," Lynn said. "If one of you can take the juice pitcher, I'll get the maple syrup. Everything else is on the table."

"Is that the real stuff?" Ed asked. "That Mrs. Whatever-her-name-is just doesn't do it for me."

"It's from a local sugar bush, actually," Lynn said. "Not ours, but local anyway. Be a dear and hold the door, won't you, please?" Ed would have to play the footman. He held the door open, sweeping them through with a gesture.

"I'll be right in with the pancakes," Alfred said. "They'll be hot, so don't touch the platter."

They filled their plates from the heaped platter situated at the head of the table, where Alfred played majordomo. Adding generous pours of maple syrup, they moved to set down plates, and pull out chairs. Lynn distributed small footed glasses of apple juice to everyone before she took her place at the far end of the table. Everyone else settled comfortably.

The door opened to the flirtation room and Norma made her entrance, sweeping in with a "Good morning, all," and a flourish of her sweater tails and scarves.

"What a grand start for a simple brunch," Harriet said.

Norma affected her play character's aplomb. "Just practicing my entrance, my dear Harriet." She flounced to the table and oozed herself into a chair, sloughing off the character as she sat. "Just to be clear, no one can call Alfred's brunch 'simple'. Always served with panache and passion."

Alfred, hand on heart, sent her a gracious dip of his head.

"Where on earth did you get this lovely fruit?" Harriet asked, sinking a serving spoon into a generous bowl of pears, peaches and grapes.

"From our orchards," Alfred said, nabbing a couple of pancakes from the platter. "We canned them last fall. Now, we get to reap the benefits."

"You really are a farmer, aren't you, Alfred?" Harriet said.

"Check for dirt under the fingernails," Ed said.

Alfred laughed. "I have a lot of help around here. Ben—you met him when he picked you up from the station—takes care of all the outside work. We like to hire locals. They do a fine job. Of course, it's plenty quiet now. But it will turn into a whirlwind of activity, come April and May."

Lynn thought, *Ben works so hard for us. He always goes above and beyond. We need to give him a nice post-New Year's bonus. I wonder if Alfred would balk at spending the money?* She sighed. *Well, if he does hesitate, I'll pay Ben out of my own funds. But let's see.* "Alfred," she said, "Ben does so very much for us around here—"

"You know," Alfred said, "you're right. I was just thinking that myself. I think we should give him a raise."

"What a wonderful idea! I wish I thought of that." Lynn hid her chuckle and sparkling eyes behind her napkin. *Of course, I did* think *of that. Thank you, Alfred.*

Harriet was busy rescuing strips of bacon from under the pancakes. "Lynn weeds after you plant, I suppose."

Ed snorted. "There's a picture. Lynn wouldn't get her perfect nails grubby, now, would she."

"You may be able to knock off some good lines, Ed Wright, but you can be a real bully sometimes," Norma said.

Ed, ignoring her, turned to Alfred. "Say, did you ever find my coat? I can't find my scarf either. I thought I might have taken it to the cottage, but it's not up there either."

"Your white aviator scarf that I got you for Christmas last year?" Harriet said.

"Yeah. I love that scarf. You didn't put it somewhere, did you?"
Harriet shook her head.

Alfred mimicked Harriet's response. "Never found your coat, Ed. I checked again this morning. I have no idea what happened to it. Tate's was still there, and the others too. It has to be around here somewhere."

"I really hate it when things disappear." Ed's voice was petulant.

Lynn stepped in to turn the conversation. "By the way, Norma, did you hear anyone stirring upstairs when you came down?"

"Not a peep."

"We were up a lot later than the girls were. I hope they don't miss Alfred's brunch."

"The fragrance of bacon and pancakes should be wafting up to them any time now," Harriet said.

At just that moment, the double doors to the flirtation room opened with a whoosh. At the table, Lynn heard a sharp cry, and everyone turned just in time to see Ellen crumple to the floor on the threshold. Behind her, Lily wasn't quick enough to catch Ellen, but did crouch down to keep Ellen from collapsing into a heap.

Lynn was out of her seat in a flash, heading for the girls.

"Ouch! I turned my ankle!" Ellen's voice betrayed approaching tears.

Harriet sprang up, almost upsetting her chair into Lynn. "Don't move her. I'll get some ice." She ran into the kitchen.

Lynn motioned for the others to stay at the table. "Give the girls some space. They don't need us getting in the way. Wait for Harriet." She leaned down to run her hands, with a gentle touch, along Ellen's ankle.

Harriet, folding over a dishtowel full of ice cubes, rushed to Ellen, who was gripping her ankle with both hands. Harriet fussed over both girls, and soon had the situation under control. "The best thing is to elevate that foot," Harriet said, reaching over to brush a strand of hair off Ellen's face. "Can you move your ankle?"

Ellen tilted her ankle in slow motion, just a slight wiggle. "I think so. It doesn't hurt too much." Her stricken face belied that optimism.

"Come on," Harriet motioned to Lily. "Let's help her into the kitchen. It'll be easier to prop up her foot there than in the dining room."

Alfred leaped up to help get Ellen upright, but the girl waved him off and put her arms across the women's shoulders.

Lynn was already opening the swinging door to the kitchen, positioning herself so they could get past her.

"This will work fine." The three hobbled off into the kitchen.

Alfred made up two plates and followed them. Soon, he and Harriet were back in the dining room. Harriet said, "Ellen assures us she'll be fine. The icepack seems to be helping already."

Lynn too slid back into her chair after checking the threshold for anything that might have tripped up Ellen. But all looked clear. "Poor dears. I hope Ellen will be all right."

"We can prop her up on the settee in the drawing room," Norma said. "She can take it easy, and run lines from there."

"Right now," Alfred said, "they're all set in the kitchen. We can finish brunch and regroup in the drawing room when we're ready. Just take your time."

"Good idea, Alfred," Lynn said. "That was a bit too much excitement to open the day, I'd say. We need a little time to settle down."

"Have another pancake," Alfred said, offering the platter to Ed.

"Thanks. I believe I will," Ed said.

"By the way, Ed," Lynn said, "did you finish the rewrites you wanted to?"

Ed whirled his hand in the air, his mouth being occupied with pancake.

"He certainly did," Harriet answered for him. "I think you all will be pleased."

"Say, where's Tate?" Alfred said.

Norma rolled her eyes. "Probably still camped out on the sofa. He didn't come up to bed." She giggled. "So, I got a really good night's sleep. Finish eating. I'll check on him when we're done. Remember, you said breakfast was *laissez-faire*, everyone for themselves if not at the table. And no pressure. But it'll serve him right if he has to eat cold pancakes."

"I'll pop some in the oven," Alfred said. "Bacon too. That should hold him until—"

"Tea time," Lynn said, her voice chiming.

"That's the British for you. I've taken up the habit, and now I don't want to give it up," Alfred said.

They didn't dawdle, but finished eating in good time. Norma went off to roust out Tate while the others cleared the table. The girls in the kitchen seemed to be recovering nicely, and Lynn helped shepherd Ellen and Lily out. They met Norma in the flirtation room. She was coming from the library.

"He's not there." Norma frowned, and set to chewing on a cuticle, before she splayed her fingers away from her face. "Bad childhood habit. When I get a bit nervous...where is Tate anyway?"

By this time, everyone was clustered in the flirtation room.

"Listen," Lynn said, "let's get Ellen onto the settee. Take weight off that twisted ankle."

They all trooped into the drawing room and settled Ellen, with Lily perched by her side.

"Now," Lynn said. "Where *is* Tate?"

"Did you try upstairs?" Ed asked Norma. "Maybe he's in the bathroom."

Off she went, but was back quickly. "Not upstairs either."

"Maybe he went for a walk," Ellen said.

"In this weather?" Lynn shivered.

"He does like to get outside to get the stink off, as he puts it," Norma said. "Maybe somebody should check outside. Find his footprints or something."

"All right, let's split up and check the house first," Alfred said. "Norma, check everywhere on this level. Ed and I can look downstairs, and Lynn, you and Harriet can check upstairs. You know all the nooks and crannies up there." He gestured around the drawing room. "You two girls just stay put. Somebody is bound to herd him back here from wherever he is."

The hunt was on.

When they regrouped in the drawing room, they all looked stymied. No sign of Tate anywhere.

"I'm going outside to see if I can find him," Alfred said. "The rest of you stay here. No reason for us all to go out in that cold. Besides, there's not that much territory to search between the main house and the cottage, and it's daylight. The storm finally stopped too." He turned to Lynn and Norma. "Why don't you two get a fire started? If Tate went outside, he'll be grateful for some heat when I find him."

Norma stoked the fire and Lynn got the fur throw from the library. They left the door open to the flirtation room, in case Tate found his way back into the house.

•   •   •

"Norma, come play a game of Scrabble with me," Lynn called. *Hopefully, it will take her mind off how slowly time crawls when you're anxious.* "Norma?"

Norma was standing at the window in the flirtation room. "I can't see Alfred."

Lynn got up and joined Norma. She motioned for Harriet to stay with the girls. When she got to the window, she shaded her eyes from the brightness of sun on snow, and peered out across the courtyard. "I can see his footprints from the house across the courtyard. There's such a glare that it's hard to see much across the lawn, but I can see where he made his way up to the cottage."

"Wait! Alfred's coming out on the cottage porch." Norma pointed out the figure making his way down the porch steps. "Where is he going?"

"He's moving toward the pool. There's a little hill there off to the right, so that will help him to see better, if he climbs up. Our grounds are all hills and valleys." *I hope he didn't fall into the pool. There's no fence, and it's deep. The way the hill is situated, the snow might go right over the pool. Or maybe there's enough down there to cushion any fall.* She didn't dare say anything out loud about the pool. She and Alfred were rarely at Ten Chimneys in the winter, and everyone knew to stay away from the concrete pool emptied for the winter.

"There! There he is!"

"Alfred clearly didn't find Tate in the cottage. He's heading for the pool. You can't see much of the pool from here. Only the very edge." Lynn didn't want Norma to see how worried she was. "But it's right behind the roofline of the poolhouse." She pointed out the red roof with its cupola, just visible over a rise of ground.

If Tate were exploring, he would tire out quickly, slogging through the snowdrifts. Yet, the estate was truly beautiful with the trees loaded with whipped cream snow, and the drifts strewn about like graceful ocean waves. That, plus the outbuildings, decorated with drifts and frost, might be enough to draw him along, in spite of the deep snow and the chilly wind. The sun was giving an illusion of warmth, if not real heat. If Tate liked to walk...

But if Tate went out while it was still dark, and veered off toward the pool... Lynn pulled her speculations tight. No one knew exactly when Tate went out. But it was clear he most certainly did go outside. He wasn't anywhere in the house.

"What's taking him so long?" Norma chewed the cuticle on her index finger, oblivious to her earlier aversion to the childhood habit.

Lynn put her arm across Norma's shoulder. "We have a lot of outbuildings here. The barn, the greenhouse." She didn't want to catalog them all. "It will take some time to check everything. It's best to be thorough, as long as he's out there."

But Alfred did not make a second appearance, though, as Lynn said, the many humps and dips on the grounds could hide someone from view, if they were in the right place. Or the wrong place, in this case.

"Come on, Norma. Come play just one game of Scrabble with me. It will make the time go faster." She turned Norma away from the window and sent her ahead to the drawing room. "I'm going to get some cocoa out for Alfred and Tate when they come in. They'll be frozen."

She took a last look out the window, intending to head for the kitchen. She caught sight of Alfred's tweed coat standing at the top of the broad concrete stairway on the end of the pool, the only part visible from where she stood. The deck was the top step, and the stairs went gradually down to the very bottom of the pool. The easiest way to get in and out. Even so, with the snow, who knew how much piled up into the pool. She was uneasy with Alfred clambering about on slippery steps, feeling his way along perhaps. She shook her head to clear it of rising unease.

She knew it was dangerous to stand still, because it might draw Norma back out, but she couldn't tear herself away.

Lynn couldn't see more than Alfred bending over before she heard Norma call from the drawing room. "Coming!" She dared not linger longer. She rushed to open the door to the main staircase, hoping she would better hear as Alfred came back.

She went into the drawing room and helped Norma set up the Scrabble board, but her mind wasn't in the game. Listening for Alfred coming into the laundry room, she missed opportunities she normally would not. Finally, she heard him come in, stomping snow off his galoshes, and rattling hangers as he hung up his coat.

Strange that not a sound more could be heard. Lynn felt cold fingers creep up her back.

Norma froze with a tile in her hand. "Alfred's back. But I don't hear Tate." She threw the tile down on the table and started to stand up.

Lynn put her hand out to stop Norma. "Wait. He's coming up."

Norma sat like a statue at the game table, and the two girls on the settee stopped murmuring to each other. Harriet was planted before the fireplace. Keeping their eyes on the open door, Ellen and Lily reached out to each other and clasped hands. Ed was staring out a window at the far end of the room. Time seemed to create a backwash.

After that quick glance around, Lynn was afraid to move.

~16~

Lynn, seeing the look on Alfred's face as he came into the drawing room, stretched to grasp Norma's hands. But too quick for Lynn, Norma rose, upsetting the Scrabble racks and sending tiles across the board and onto the floor. She took a step, but then joined the tableau formed by the others.

Alfred was clutching...something...in both hands. "Ed." He cleared his throat. "I...I have something."

Ed strode to meet Alfred. He reached out and took what Alfred was offering him. "You found my scarf." He seemed unable to say more.

Alfred went to Norma and took her hands.

"Where's Tate?" Norma never took her eyes from Alfred. "What happened?"

Alfred shook his head, and Lynn moved to Norma and put an arm across her shoulders.

"I'm sorry, Norma. I don't know how to put this," Alfred said. "I found Tate."

Lynn heard Norma take a deep breath in and hold it.

"In the pool," Alfred said. "I'm so sorry. He's dead, Norma. There was nothing I could do."

Harriet moved to Ed and tried to take the scarf from him, but it unfurled between them. Harriet withdrew her hands, a look of horror on her face.

Norma's cry rent the air. Her gaze swiveled to Ed. It was impossible to miss the splashes of red blood on the scarf he held. "No. No!" She tried to pull her hands from Alfred's grip, but he held tight, pulling her toward him. With Lynn at her back, they were able to support her to a nearby chair, where she collapsed. She put her hands up to hide her face, but made not a sound.

Ed's hands trembled as he folded the scarf into a small packet so the blood wasn't visible. Offering it back to Alfred, he said, "You take it. I don't want it anymore."

Alfred took it and shoved it in his pocket.

Lynn looked at Alfred, who only shook his head. *Tate is dead?* she thought. *Found in the pool?* Her thoughts spooled off to the storm, losing his way, one misstep, and... She couldn't bear to think of it. Even as Harriet rushed to kneel in front of Norma, shushing and clucking, Lynn pulled Alfred aside. "He's gone, I see that. What happened? Can you tell? Did you...did you leave him there?"

"No, no." Alfred drew her into an embrace. "Of course not. I got him into the poolhouse. He's a big man, but I could slide him on the snow. It's cold and the...he'll be fine there until we can get someone out here."

"Do you think someone *can* get out here?"

"Not the way the roads are now. Everything appears to be blocked. And some trees are down as well, the wind was so strong last night."

"Did a tree perhaps fall on him?" Lynn asked.

Alfred frowned. "We have only one birch down, and it's nowhere near the pool. I think he went out last night, lost his way in the storm, and fell into the pool. He was head down at the bottom of the steps." He shook his head and pursed his lips. "But why? Why was he out?"

"Just what I was about to ask," Lynn said. "But right now, we need to pay attention to Norma." They turned back to the chair, now surrounded by Harriet, Lily, even Ellen, who hobbled over to join them. Ed hovered above the women. Lynn and Alfred joined them.

"So why did he have my scarf?" Ed said.

"What do you mean?" Norma said, sitting up and locking gazes with Ed. She needed answers, surely, even more than the rest of them did.

"Whenever he went out," Alfred said, "he must've left the laundry room dark, and just grabbed his coat without turning the lights on. He must have snagged your scarf by mistake, Ed."

"That's crazy," Ed said, clearly not paying attention to Norma's discomfort.

But Norma wanted answers, apparently. She ignored Ed. "Why did he go out in the first place? And when? We left him in the library. I never heard him leave."

Lynn knew Tate could easily leave the library undetected if he went through the little hallway by the bathroom and out into the flirtation room. From there, he could simply get downstairs by the main stairs, to the laundry room, and outside. Easy enough to avoid Ed in the kitchen that way too. From what she saw—the fall into the pool, in particular—pointed to Tate leaving the house sometime during the storm. Why else would he be so far off track?

But *why*? Why was he out in the first place? That was the most important question.

"Why? *Why*?!" Norma asked the same question over and over.

No one had an answer.

"We may never know," Alfred said. "Maybe he just needed some fresh air."

"In the middle of the storm?" Apparently, Norma came to the same conclusion as Lynn: Tate walked off the edge of the pool in confusion, lost in the blowing snow. Norma shook her head. "He wouldn't go out in such weather. He was far too practical. He was an accountant, for God's sake, not an Arctic explorer!" She began to weep.

Lynn turned to her husband. "Alfred, can you go back out while it's still sunny, and see if you can find anything else? See if there's something in the pool where the...where you found him."

"Of course," Alfred said. "Maybe there's something to help explain why he went out."

"Can somebody figure out how to get blood out of my scarf?" Ed asked.

What a petty thing to worry about at such a time, Lynn thought. But she said nothing.

Alfred turned to leave the room. Lynn followed him out. "I'll see if the phone lines are working," she said, "though I have my doubts. What a horrible thing to happen."

Alfred squeezed her hand. "If we have to stay isolated here until they can get to us, we'll be fine. Even Tate...his body will be safe in the poolhouse. Nothing can get in, and the cold will keep him...safe."

Lynn nodded. "Safe, yes. Well. Search the pool carefully, Alfred. Norma needs to know what happened, as close as we can tell."

A lift of the phone receiver confirmed that they were stranded. At least they had heat and electricity. But no way to contact the outside world until the roads were cleared and the phone service restored. They'd have to make the best of it. Which probably wouldn't be very good at all, given that one of their group was now dead. What a horrible way to go, stumbling around in the snow and the dark, never seeing the danger of a nine-foot deep concrete pool. Cracking his head open... Lynn shuddered. The blood on the scarf confirmed that.

•   •   •

Alfred was gone long enough that, when he returned, his face was rosy with cold. His hands, when he took hold of Lynn's, were icy, in spite of the gloves he wore when he went out. One look told Lynn not to ask questions.

Alfred went to Norma and knelt in front of her, grasping her clasped hands. "I made sure the coat was covering him. He's safe in the poolhouse. As soon as the phone lines are open again, we'll call for help."

"Can't we get out? Walk out or something?" Norma's voice sounded desperate.

Alfred shook his head. "The drifts are simply so deep that even the plows apparently can't get through yet. I didn't see or hear anything out and about, at least." He stood and turned to the others. "The wind is picking up again. The clouds are moving in, and it looks like more snow."

"I think we need tea," Lynn said. "Alfred, will you help me, please?" She shook her head when the others offered assistance. "No, you stay here. We'll put some biscuits and tea together. That will hold us for the moment."

When they reached the kitchen, Lynn checked the telephone. Nothing. She hung up and drew Alfred close. "I know you have something else, Alfred. I could see it in your eyes. Please tell me."

"There was an awful lot of blood, Lynnie. A lot more than from a fall, I thought. But then, head wounds can bleed furiously."

"What else did you find, Alfred? There must be something else. Something, anything."

Alfred pursed his lips and shook his head. "Nothing in the pool that I could find. No tree branch that might have come down and caused him to stumble and fall. I checked the edge of the pool above where the...body fell. But what the wind didn't sweep away, the snow covered. No footprints or signs of him slipping."

"Did you check where you found him in the pool?" Lynn was sure he did, but had to ask anyway. Double-checking never hurt.

"Yes, I went down the steps again and searched carefully. I even pushed the snow away from where the body lay. But the way the wind swirled around, most of the snow was piled up on the opposite side of the pool, and even some of the steps were visible. Whatever happened, I found the most blood in the pool, though it looked like there was some along the edge, and even down along the snow. It looked like he was bleeding as he fell." Alfred grimaced. "Most of the blood was frozen. He must have gone out last night sometime. Nothing was fresh."

"But most of the blood was at the bottom of the pool, where he landed?" Lyn grimaced at the thought.

"Lots," Alfred said. "There was a large pool of blood in the depression caused by his head. When I dragged him out of the pool, it left a wide swath behind. But much of the blood was in that depression. Far too much for him to survive. Even if we could get to him shortly after he fell, we certainly could not have saved him. Between the fall and the bleeding and..."

"It happened that quickly then." Lynn could hardly imagine the devastating fall that would crack Tate's head open to bleed so profusely. Alone, unconscious in the snow. Even with all the drifting, it wasn't enough to cushion Tate's fall. His head... She couldn't complete the thought, it was just too horrible, too gruesome.

Alfred pulled Lynn farther into the kitchen. "I went back into the pool house. Something felt wrong. There was so much blood. Too much for just a fall. So, I checked his head thoroughly." He leaned closer to her. "There was no head wound, Lynnie. But there was a great gash across his neck. Along one side, cutting the carotid. That's where the blood came from."

"What are you saying, Alfred?"

"Someone cut him, slashed him, Lynnie. He didn't just fall in the pool. He was murdered."

Lynn set her fingertips on the table for control. Her mind whirled like a kaleidoscope. "What? Why?" She bit her lip. "Alfred?"

<h1 style="text-align:center">-17-</h1>

Lynn was dumbstruck. Murder. Why Tate, ordinary Tate, accountant? When? Well, that was easy enough. Sometime during the night. But that hardly answered anything. Worthless, or perhaps not. Perhaps it said that an outsider...

Lynn shook her head to clear it. She took hold of Alfred's sleeve. "We must not say anything about our suspicions. There's too much at stake here. We're trapped without communication, or any way to get help. We need to make sure everyone stays safe until–"

"Until we can get the sheriff here," Alfred finished. "You're right. And we should keep this quiet, in case it's...someone here. Just take care that we stick together. As far as anyone else knows, Tate was disoriented by the storm, got too close to the edge, and–"

"One misstep," Lynn said. "A slip, a fall, a broken... An accident. We must not make any further guesses for the time being."

Alfred nodded his agreement.

This was not the time for speculation. This was only the time for preparing tea. The others were waiting in the drawing room. She and Alfred held crucial information. But now was not the time to share anything important. Lynn would leave that decision up to Alfred. They had to perhaps reveal something, however. They were gone too long from the drawing room already. One thing was certain, she and Alfred needed to stick together, literally. But first things first.

She began to pull out tray, pot, cups, tea, strainer, a biscuit tin, all the things needed. Alfred set about heating the kettle.

Lynn talked as she worked. "You and I need to talk through all of this. One important thing: we must get Ed and Harriet down to the main house. If there's a murderer loose around here, we need to stay together. I would never forgive myself if someone broke into the cottage and..." She set her fingers on her lips and sent Alfred a stricken look.

"Agreed. We've got the room, and no one will be alone."

"We need to really analyze this," Lynn said.

"Yes, but not now," Alfred said. "When we get everyone settled for the night, we'll have time to sort things out. Or at least try. But not right now."

Lynn nodded. "Of course. Right now, we've got to get back in with everybody."

Alfred, balancing the teapot, held the door open for Lynn. They rattled their way to the drawing room. Lily was sitting on the floor at Norma's feet. Ed and Harriet hovered close by, while Ellen was back on the settee, her foot propped up on a needlepointed pillow.

"I'll leave the tea tray over here by the piano," Lynn said, setting down the tray with a clink and positioning the cozy over the teapot, the spout sticking out like an elephant's trunk. She poured a cup and went to Norma, setting a hand on her shoulder.

Norma seemed to be in a catatonic state, but roused at Lynn's touch and took the offered cup. Too much in shock to thank or do anything but sip. She held the cup close to her face, as if the steam could obscure her stricken look.

"We tried the phone again," Lynn said, "but the lines are still down. We'll keep trying." She saw Norma shivering, so she grabbed the fur throw and draped it across Norma's knees. Alfred went discretely to the library door and closed it.

"I...We are all so very sorry about Tate. If there is anything..." Lynn knew there was nothing anyone could truly do.

"I want to see him." Norma set down her teacup and turned to Alfred. She clenched her hands on the arms of the chair. "Alfred, I need to see him. I'm going to the poolhouse." She began to rise, but Lynn rushed to her and knelt in front of her, preventing her from getting up.

"That's not possible right now, Norma." Lynn put on her most gentle voice, even though her heart was pounding. "The snow, the cold, plus you're in shock right now. The best thing is to take just a little time before you see...him." Norma could not, by any means, see the body now. She and Alfred needed to sort a few more things out. "I know, this is pure torture, Norma, but please–"

"Lynn's right," Alfred came in. "Give yourself a chance to think clearly and be at your best."

Lynn knew he was grasping at straws, but they simply couldn't let Norma go to the poolhouse. Not yet, anyway. She reached out and squeezed one of Norma's hands. "And it's getting darker outside. We wouldn't want any more accidents." She let that thought hang in the air, hoping she planted a seed that led the others away from thinking of murder.

"You were a lucky woman," Alfred said. Lynn recognized an attempted diversion. "Tate was a special man. You made a perfect couple."

Norma looked up, visibly shifting gears. "He was the love of my life. I can't believe he's gone." She shuddered, one hand stroking the fur throw without seeming to feel the soft nap. She stopped, looked up and scanned the room, as if searching for Tate. "I was working at the Goodman Theater in Chicago. He was working on accounting at Central City College. We met at a party. Actresses were always welcome, because people thought we added a bit of glamor." Norma showed a wry smile. "I could barely live on what I made at Goodman. But I could borrow an old costume, so I always looked a lot better than some of the others. I went to every party I could, because there was bound to be food. I learned early on to carry the largest beaded purse I could find. Tate caught me...stocking up." She set down her cup of tea and put her hands to her face.

Lynn was glad to see her mind spool off to the past. That was something they could all share, those hard early times. "Did he turn you in?"

Norma curled her hands in her lap. "No. He asked me to dinner the next night. Funny thing was, he hardly had two dimes to rub together himself." She took a deep breath. "He said he was in Chicago to re-invent himself. He lived somewhere in Oregon. Managed a department store. It was a rather deadend job, he said, because the son would inherit the business. So, he came to Chicago. He wanted more."

"He clearly got it when he won you," Alfred said.

Norma's lips rose, but without joy. "Once Tate had his diploma, he got a job offer in New York. It's a small firm, but the perfect size for him. He didn't want a dog-eat-dog accounting corporation." She sighed. "He asked me to marry him and move to the city with him."

Lynn said, "We're so glad you came to New York. We watched your reputation grow in Chicago, and you really got some plum roles once you moved to the city."

Norma nodded. "We went from a one room studio in Chicago to a one-bedroom, with a separate kitchen and an in-house bathroom. Quite an improvement." She looked up, her eyes filling with tears. "For Tate, I would live in a tent in Central Park." She broke down crying.

The others sat, looking stunned, but silent.

Lynn stepped into the gap. "Speaking of sleeping arrangements, I don't think we should be separate tonight," she said. "Harriet, why don't you and Ed move down to the main house with the rest of us? We need to support one another."

"Great idea," Ed put in. He was standing at a window, watching the weather. "It's starting to snow again."

"I'm going up to lie down for a while," Norma said, as if just realizing she reached the end of her rope. She pressed Lily away from her, and moved to get up. Giving a gasp, she dropped back into the chair.

Alarm rippled through the others. Was Norma ill? "Are you all right?" Harriet asked.

"I can't bear to go into that room," Norma wailed.

Ellen sat up and swung her legs onto the floor. "Wait, Norma. You can stay in my room. It's small, but it's cozy, and you can rest."

"But where will you go then?" Lily asked.

"If Ed and Harriet are coming down here, why don't they take Ta—Norma's room? Norma can have mine," Ellen said, "and…well, if you don't mind, I could bunk in with you, Lily. You have a bigger bed." She raised her eyebrows in an unspoken question at Lily.

"Perfect," Lily said.

Lynn breathed a sigh of relief. "Yes, perfect," she echoed. "Alfred, why don't you and Ed go up to the cottage and collect everything." She went to the window and peered out. "The wind is picking up again. If we're going to be snowed in tighter, we might as well all be together."

"Great idea, Lynnie," Alfred said. "Come on, Ed. If we go right now, we can avoid the worst of this storm." They headed downstairs to bundle up.

"Don't forget my nightgown, Ed," Harriet called after them. "It's under my pillow."

"I think I'm okay to walk," Ellen said, testing her ankle with a few steps. "Let's go upstairs, Lily, and move my things out, so Norma can rest. Come with us, Norma. You can check out my little room."

Norma accepted Lily's offer of a hand, and rose to intertwine her arms with the girls'. They set off.

When they were gone, Harriet turned to Lynn. "Looks like it's just us, Lynn. Thank you for suggesting we move down here. I'm not sure I want to be alone up there, between the snow and…"

"I understand," Lynn said. "We've plenty of room. With the girls together and Norma in the little bedroom, you and Ed can have…the other room. It's got a roomy double bed." *I wouldn't spend a moment alone either, what with a murderer out there somewhere.* That thought froze her bones. They needed to keep themselves busy. "Let's go to the library. When I went in, papers were stacked everywhere. Tate was apparently organizing things. You and I can gather things together, so Norma doesn't have to deal with that too."

"Good idea," Harriet said.

They went up to the library. It was much as they left it the night before, except by this time, Tate had spread paperwork on the sofa and the chair, and on almost every other horizontal surface. Harriet stood in the doorway, as if to avoid touching anything important. Lynn bit her tongue on the spontaneous thought of murder.

She laid a fresh fire and lit the crumple of paper she stuffed under the logs. She brushed her hands together and looked around. "Where shall we start?" It was a weak comment, but enough to get them both moving.

"Here's his briefcase." Harriet stepped into the room, lifted the briefcase off the floor and set it on the desk chair. "I don't have the faintest idea what all this stuff is about, so I guess we can just stack it and even up the edges to put in the briefcase. It looks big enough to hold it all."

"You're right. There's not a lot, but it's spread all over." Lynn went to the sofa and persuaded a scattering of loose papers into a pile. She turned to go after the briefcase. "You haven't worked with Norma before?"

Harriet stood in front of Alfred's big overstuffed chair, hands on hips. With her back to Lynn, she was impossible to read. But she pulled her shoulders down and held her head high. The rigidity was brief, but it puzzled Lynn. The body language said...what? At the very least, disturbance, perhaps even anger. Lynn opted not to pursue that thought. "Here's the first load." She slid her pile of papers into the briefcase and went to the end table for more, making sure to stand so she could see Harriet. Something...

"What?" Harriet said, clearly distracted. "No, we haven't worked with Norma. I know of her reputation. I...Ed wanted to see if she was under contract, because he had a play in mind for her." Harriet picked up the stack of booklets on the chair and turned. "I wonder if these will fit. We might have to find a box."

Lynn, always aware of movements, words, gestures to incorporate in her roles, was sure she felt mounting tension in Harriet. More to make small talk than anything, she said, "Tate seemed congenial enough. It's clear Norma and he got along famously."

Harriet dropped into the chair behind her, letting loose the pile of booklets in her arms. They slithered down to pool on the carpet at her feet. Before Lynn got a look at her face, Harriet's hands were up, shielding her face completely.

"Harriet! Are you okay?" Lynn set down papers and went to her.

"I'm glad he's dead." Barely a whisper.

But Lynn heard. Her lips formed *What?*, but she did not speak it aloud. Did not dare to. She crouched on the carpet, ready to set a hand on Harriet's knee. Yet, she held back. The two women formed a silent pair.

Finally, Lynn whispered, "I'm sure you don't mean that, Harriet."

Harriet unleashed a stream of invective that seemed totally out of character, followed by, "I'm *glad* he's dead! I am! He deserved to die!" From there, she spooled out the story. "A plastic surgeon. That's what he was when I knew him. A plastic surgeon."

A flash crossed Lynn's mind. "The car accident."

"Oh, no, Lynn. Not the car accident." Harriet took her hands down and grasped the chair's arms. Her fingers turned white, she clutched so tight. "Yes, I was in a car accident. Yes, I needed a plastic surgeon." She indicated the right side of her face.

Lynn frowned. "I don't understand." The right side of Harriet's face was crushed, the eye orbit pulled aside, the cheekbone caved in, scars like creeks and rivers.

Harriet gave out a crooked smile, but her eyes were burning with anger. She nodded. "Yes, it's still a mess, isn't it? He–Tate–did nothing. Nothing. And when Tate the surgeon was finished with me, nobody else could do anything either."

Lynn was stunned into silence.

"But he didn't exactly do nothing. That's not really true either. See this?" Harriet ran her finger along the livid scar stretching from temple to chin on the left side. "This was Tate's scalpel. Can you believe that?"

"Oh, Harriet." It was all Lynn could muster.

"He was drunk, Lynn. *Drunk!* He came to operate on me drunk! No one knew. He was such a closet alcoholic that he was *always* drunk. They said they couldn't even smell anything on him. He collapsed in the operating room, and dragged his knife right down my face as he fell." Harriet put her hands to her face again. Her shoulders shook as she cried silently.

Lynn did reach out then, with a gentle touch to Harriet's arm. "I'm so sorry, Harriet. I had no idea. Does Ed know?"

Harriet took her hands down and nodded. She sniffed and pulled her shoulders back, straightening her posture. "I told him years ago. But at the time it happened, no one knew." Harriet bit her lip. "I sued Tate for everything I could get and left California. The lawyers took care of everything. No one had to look at me. The judge met with me, and then excused me from the trial. It was just too traumatic for me, and everyone saw that. I did manage to read the transcript much, much later. Apparently, according to the nurses' testimony, he was flailing around the room that day, and finally almost fell across me, and the scalpel…" She put her fingers on her lips.

"I am so very sorry," Lynn said. "I wish there was something I could do, Harriet."

Harriet sent her a crooked smile. "He didn't even remember being in the operating room that morning. Can you believe that? He only saw photos later of the damage he did. Then, he still kept denying it."

"So, he doesn't know who you are?" Lynn asked.

"He didn't recognize me when we walked into the kitchen here." Her face took on a look of thunder. "But I recognized him."

-18-

Lynn heard Ed and Alfred come in downstairs, slam the outside door, then shuffle off galoshes and coats. Muffled conversation continued as the men went directly up to the bedroom where Harriet and Ed would sleep.

By the time the men clattered downstairs and into the drawing room, Lynn was back from the library. She left Harriet in the big chair in the library, saying to her, "Don't rush, dear. Just compose yourself and come in when you're ready. I think Ellen and Lily are still upstairs rearranging things for themselves." She closed the door behind her, and was sitting in one of the chairs before the fireplace when Ed and Alfred came in. Time enough later to tell Alfred what she learned.

Lily and Ellen appeared at the door right behind the men. "We got everyone moved, Miss Fontanne," Ellen said.

"I think Norma is sleeping," Lily said. "It was pretty quiet on that end of the hall."

"It's best we allow her some privacy," Lynn said. "The shock is terrible." She kept any other thoughts to herself. She needed to talk with Alfred. Things were getting complicated.

"I see you girls stoked the fire," Alfred said, going over and stretching his hands out toward the flames. "Thanks for that. The wind is bitter cold out there. I'm glad we don't have to go out in it again."

"We checked the telephone when we came up through the kitchen," Ed said. "No go."

"If the wind kicks up even more, they won't be able to get the lines up. Too dangerous for the linemen," Alfred said.

"Maybe it'll get better tomorrow," Ellen said. Her teeth were chattering.

"Go stand by Alfred, darling," Lynn said to her. "You look like you're freezing."

The door opened to the library. "All the papers are in...the briefcase," Harriet said, coming down into the drawing room. "I left it on the chair by the desk."

Lynn was encouraged by Harriet's calm demeanor. Completely under control. Lynn knew enough to keep everything from the library to herself. If Harriet wanted to tell anyone else about her car accident and Tate's subsequent involvement, or not, that was Harriet's prerogative. Right now, she and Alfred were gathering evidence, so the less information spread around, the better.

"I'm glad we decided to stay together," Lynn said, "here in the drawing room." Which elicited a glance from Alfred. She could read questions in his look, but she knew no one else could. "I feel so much better surrounded by all of you." That was certainly the truth. She had plenty of questions swirling around her own mind, but didn't want to voice a single one until she could closet with Alfred. That obviously wouldn't happen until they all went to bed. Well, so be it. She could play the good hostess. She could play any role she needed to, under the circumstances.

Ellen voiced what probably most of them were thinking. "Now what? What should we do?"

"Well," Lynn began, "we can take some time to read through that second scene that was giving us so much trouble back in New York."

The perfect cue for Alfred. "A very good idea, Lynnie. Tate is safe, Norma is resting. She doesn't need to be surrounded by anxious people when she comes down. So, the rest of us can use this time to calm ourselves. Norma will need real friends."

Based on the general positive murmurings, everyone agreed. The read-throughs would keep them busy for a good part of the afternoon and allow them to move Tate's death to the background for a little while, at least.

Lily said, "No guarantee I'll remember a single word, but it seems the best thing to do for the time being." She moved to a chair closer to the group and sat down, tucking her feet up under her.

Ellen nodded. She shuffled through the scripts on the table, found hers, and perched on a step to the library. She backed up against the wall and opened the booklet. "I'll be right here."

Ed picked up his and Norma's scripts. "Harriet can read Norma's lines." The two of them commandeered the blue settee. Harriet put her feet up and snuggled against Ed's shoulder, her legs slid under the throw at the end of the settee.

Lynn caught a pointed look from Alfred, but she shook her head—one quick movement. She knew he got the message that now was not the time to talk about anything. With what she learned from Harriet, coupled with the knowledge about the cut on Tate's neck, she thought... Well, she truly didn't know what to think. There would be time later. No one was going anywhere.

To settle her nerves and focus, she tucked her script under her arm, and made the rounds of the room, striding with a purpose that didn't seem to exist. She went to a chair in front of the fireplace and sank down. "There. A bit of exercise, and I can concentrate on the scene now." Alfred draped himself in the chair opposite her. In spite of his relaxed look, Alfred was, Lynn knew, ready to focus. Once they were alone, they would have the time to sort some of this out. Until then, time to bear down and put their minds on the task at hand.

They ran through the scene over and over, a few lines at a time, making adjustments as they went. Voice inflections, what to emphasize, how to position themselves. They picked the scene apart, line by line, then put it back together again. Sometimes it worked, sometimes it didn't. Ed took notes in such a furious hand, Lynn wondered if he'd be able to decipher his scratchings later.

Sometime close to noon, Alfred disappeared, reappearing shortly with a tray stacked with sandwiches, fruit, and drink. He made a second trip to bring out plates, napkins, and utensils on a second tray, which he set up on Lynn's gaming table, out of the way of the central action. "If anyone gets hungry, you don't have far to go. Please, help yourselves."

The afternoon played out like a slow-motion dance at times. People drifted from one spot to another, perching on the edge of a chair, watching out a window, sometimes eating, warming with a back to the fire, pacing back and forth, plopping down on settee or chair or piano bench. Other times, it was more like a flamenco, with actors bending rhythmically toward each other, precise with sharp movements.

During a break in her lines, Lynn went up to the library and brought an armful of magazines to help give a bit of diversity—and diversion—to the afternoon to those who weren't in a particular part of the scene.

She heard only snatches of script dialogue here and there, as they all, eventually, turned to concentrate on their own separate parts. Soon, no one seemed willing to broach normal conversation with another human being.

As shadows lengthened into blue twilight, and the sun sank below the tree level, Lynn grew restless. She rose and sighed. "It's getting late, Alfred. Would you consider putting together something for a light supper? We worked hard, and it's past teatime." She gave a short chuckle. "Though I can always enjoy a cuppa…" Of course, she knew why the usual rhythms were all askew. Tate.

Alfred, quick to rescue her, said, "We have beef stew left, and I brought a loaf of cardamom bread when we came out. I'll make more coffee and tea. Maybe some cocoa too."

"Do we have anything for dessert?" Ed asked. "I hear you make the best desserts."

Maybe it was his attempt to regain some normalcy, but whatever the reason, Lynn felt unexpectedly grateful. The weight on her shoulders slipped off just a little.

"I'll pull strawberries out of the freezer right now and set them on the stove where it's warm, so they're thawed before we want them," Alfred said. "There's a sponge cake out there too, and that should suffice." Over his shoulder as he left for the kitchen, he added, "I'll double check what else Ben's wife loaded up the fridge with."

"Let's move to the dining room," Lynn said. "I don't know about anyone else, but I need a change of scene."

They all stood at that pronouncement, apparently just as eager as she was. Conversation began, dribbling at first, but expanding to a give and take, a flow of small talk to cushion the circumstances of Tate's death, even if Norma was still upstairs and unable to hear them.

When they reached the dining room, Lynn brought out a bottle of wine and glasses. Ed opened the wine and poured everyone a generous serving. Alfred appeared with a tray of cheese, crackers, and a tin of paté. "This will hold off the demon hunger. And no one needs to drink wine on an empty stomach."

"Mr. Lunt?"

Alfred stopped with his hand on the swinging door into the kitchen. "What is it, Lily?"

"If you make up something for Norma, I'll take it up to her and sit with her for a while. If that's all right."

"That's a wonderful idea," Lynn said. "Thank you, Lily."

"Let us know if she knows why..." Ellen put her fingers on her mouth and her eyes widened. "I'm sorry," she whispered.

"It's okay, kid," Ed said. "It's what we're all wondering."

Before long, the beef stew was heated, the bread sliced and the table set. Everyone settled in to eat.

Lily, with food and utensils for herself and Norma, headed upstairs.

-19-

After supper, they all lingered in the dining room, everyone clearly unwilling to be alone. Ellen went up to check on Norma and Lily. She came back down, and stood at the dining room door, to report that Norma fell asleep holding Lily's hand. For her part, Lily was still upstairs, having, according to Ellen, decided to retire to bed with a book. She promised to stay up and wait for Ellen before turning off the light. Ellen said her good nights and returned upstairs.

Conversation among the remaining two couples began with weather, stalled, went on to speculation of what friends were doing in New York, stalled, picked up with commentary on Ed's rewrites, stalled, petered out after praise for Alfred's cooking, and finally ground to a complete halt. They headed up to bed.

Lynn sat down at her dressing table and proceeded to remove her makeup. She patted moisturizer on her face and neck, closing her eyes and calming herself. She added hand cream, checking her cuticles and massaging each finger with a gentle touch. After slipping on a warm flannel nightgown, she turned off the lights in the dressing room.

When she emerged in the bedroom, she found Alfred standing barefoot, in his pajamas, with a slipper in each hand, staring off into space. "Alfred, whatever are you doing?"

"What? Oh." He emerged from a reverie. "I just have a terrible feeling that I'm missing something. What am I missing?" He scratched his head with a slipper.

"But you checked everything, Alfred. What could you possibly be missing?" Lynn said.

"I don't know, Lynnie. I even took the time to check out everyone's boots and galoshes, but the laundry room is so cold anyway, they were all still wet from the snow. They couldn't tell me who went out, or when, because even yours were wet and you haven't been out since we got here."

There was a brief moment of silence, involving a lot of frowning, and then they swiveled to each other, eyebrows raised. "Pockets!" they said in unison.

"You didn't check his pockets," Lynn said. "Did you? Did you check his pockets?"

"No! That's it, Lynnie." Alfred dropped his slippers to the floor. "I was too focused on all that blood. And then, when I went into the poolhouse to check on him, I saw the slice on his neck and everything else went right out the window. I came back to the house to tell you."

Lynn nodded. "Pockets. Maybe there's something in one of his pockets."

"I'm going out right now and check that out," Alfred said. When she started to protest, he stopped her. "I can find my way up easily. I'll just backtrack through my footprints in the snowbanks. They've been walked in twice now, so it'll be easy."

"Take a torch, Alfred," Lynn said. "You can turn it on when you get in the poolhouse. No one will see it from the house. There are no windows on that side." Her story would keep until he returned.

"Good idea," Alfred said. By that time, he already had his pants on over his pajama bottoms. After tucking in the pajama top, he cinched the belt tight. He pulled his socks on again. "My boots and coat are in the laundry room, so I can make a silent getaway." Stopping at the door, he turned and whispered, "I'll be right back."

"Alfred." Lynn stopped him with her whisper. "Check his pants pockets too. He may have something hidden there that he would want with him wherever he went. Something that would draw a murderer to him. Someone who wanted whatever Tate had."

Alfred sent her a salute. He opened the bedroom door and did a discrete check of the hall before slipping out and closing the door behind him, all without a sound.

Lynn crawled into bed, but sat with her arms wrapped around her drawn-up knees. She waited.

She set her forehead on her knees, and concentrated on deep breathing. In through the nose, out through the mouth. She waited, reviewing the story Harriet told her. If Harriet killed Tate for revenge, how did she get him out of the library? Out of the house? Would there be a note from Harriet in one of his pockets? All of that speculation would have to wait until Alfred returned. She sighed.

Lifting up her head, she stretched out her legs, and reached for her toes. And waited some more.

She was almost out of patience when the bedroom door opened, sliver by sliver, and Alfred slipped in.

She raised her eyebrows.

He set a finger on his lips, pulled a paper out of his trouser pocket, and set it on the nightstand. He loosened his belt and let his trousers slide to the floor. Leaving them there, not his usual neat response, he slid into bed next to Lynn without taking off his socks. He radiated cold.

Lynn was not about to complain. She cuddled up next to him, drawing the blanket up over both of them. Then she waited. Again.

"You'll never believe what I found, Lynnie," Alfred said apparently warmed enough so his teeth didn't chatter. He sat up, reached out and retrieved the paper from the nightstand. "This." Alfred held out a folded piece of paper. He held it up so she could see "Harriet" written on the front.

She frowned. "Where did you find this? In his coat pocket?"

"No," Alfred said. "You were right. It was in his pants pocket. There was nothing in his coat pockets other than gloves, so, I opened the coat and looked in every pocket I could reach."

"Did you read the note?" With the note addressed to Harriet, how could it be anything but important?

"No, I just stuck it in my pocket, and hurried back here. I didn't want to read it until we could read it together." He slithered back down to lie next to her. "I'm still cold!"

Lynn snuggled close to Alfred. "Open it. We need to know if it's worth killing for."

Alfred opened the note, while she looked over his shoulder. They read in silence. When they reached the end, they exchanged looks.

"There's something I need to tell you, Alfred. I wanted to wait until we were alone." Lynn related the story Harriet told her in the library. The car accident, the drunk plastic surgeon, the permanent damage. The name of the doctor. Dr. Tate Alexander. Her initial suspicions about Harriet.

By the time she finished, Alfred went from prone to propped up on one elbow, his attention focused on her every word. He gave a low whistle. "That throws an entirely different light on this, doesn't it?"

"We need to process what we've discovered. The note isn't as clear as it could be."

"Agreed," Alfred said, leaning over, ready to slide the paper under the bed, where it would be safe until morning.

Lynn set a hand on his back. "Wait. Read it again, Alfred. Read it out loud, please."

Alfred sat up, the note still in his hand. "Yes, good."

She nodded. "We need to spend as much time on this as we do on a script. I need to hear it again. But whisper, darling, just whisper." She moved close to him.

"All right, Lynnie. You're right." Alfred unfolded the note and began reading, his voice barely audible. "'Harriet. I'm writing this in case you won't see me. I want you to know how terrible I feel, and how sorry. And how guilty. I never meant to hurt you. I was an alcoholic-no, I was a drunk, a falling-down drunk, and I did awful things to you. I can never make up to you what's been done, but I need you to see me as I am now: clean for many years. No longer a doctor either. After that horrible day, I never touched anything medical again. I became a new person. I know you can never forget. I can't either. I can't forgive myself. But I hope you can understand, if not forgive. You don't need to forgive me, or even acknowledge my existence, but I hope this note can help lessen some of your pain. I truly am sorry. Tate Alexander.'"

"But he still had the note," Lynn said. "That could mean a number of things."

Alfred folded the note and tucked it under the bed. He lay down and looped his arm beneath her shoulders.

She scooched tight against him and lay her head on his shoulder. "I'm terrified, Alfred. Terrified and confused."

"Let's do the terrified first," Alfred said. "Start with the basics. You're terrified, of course, because there are two possibilities: someone from outside, or someone in the house. We have to be objective enough to consider both. We're not absolutely sure who killed Tate. It could be someone from outside, a random strike, not targeted."

"If that's the case-and I don't think it is-we can't even warn anyone, or call for help, because the phone lines are down, and the snow is too deep to walk all the way into town."

"That scene means we can't really do anything but lock up the house tight." Alfred squeezed her gently. "Which I did already, and even double checked as I went. So, that is not a solution to be terrified about, I think."

"You're right. But if it's not an outsider..." She looked up at him.

"Then it's someone inside."

Lynn wrinkled her forehead. "You can't be thinking it's..." She shook her head. "I can't believe she'd do something like that."

"Who knows what drives anyone to such measures?" There was no real answer for that. "There was certainly opportunity."

"And more, the way it looks," Lynn said. "The note was...well, we mustn't draw conclusions from it. Not yet, anyway. We need to know more."

"I agree," Alfred said. "We need more information. But what, exactly?"

"Setting that aside for the moment, it seems more likely that the murderer is among us. That *is* something to be terrified about."

Alfred shook his head. "Not necessarily. If so, then the murder was not random."

"So," Lynn sat up and turned to face Alfred, kneeling next to him. "Someone deliberately killed Tate."

Alfred lifted himself up on one elbow. "I don't know, Lynnie. I really don't know." He lay back down and gestured for her to join him. "But I think it's something we need to keep to ourselves for the time being. We can't have a general panic. Good, if everyone leans toward an outsider killing Tate. Better, if it's considered an accident, an unfortunate accident when Tate slipped and fell." He settled back onto the pillows.

Lynn stretched out again, her head in the crook of his arm and a hand on his chest. "Why was Tate out in the first place." It was hardly a question. "He had the note addressed to Harriet. Maybe he never made it up to the cottage, the way it looks."

"Well, we can't even be sure of that," Alfred said. "You may be right. But he could have gotten to the cottage and delivered his message in person to Harriet. If that's the case, there would be no need to hand off the note. He wrote in the note that it was composed in case she wouldn't see him. So, perhaps he talked with Harriet, and was on his way back to the main house when he was killed."

"Oh, Alfred, this is getting more and more complex," Lynn said. "All right. Start with the murder then, not with the why or how. Well, we know the how. His throat was slashed. But using what? We don't know." She shivered and slid closer to Alfred.

"Who then?" Alfred said. "Who could get out in that storm? Let's consider everyone."

"Well, Tate got out, that's for certain. He could leave the library the back way, go down the main stairs and be gone and back before–"

"But he never made it back," Alfred said.

She didn't need reminding. "But who could leave to commit murder, and then get back in?"

"Almost anyone," Alfred said. "Harriet could leave the cottage easily enough, and we would never know."

"Ed could leave the kitchen too, go down the back stairs and out, and we wouldn't hear him either."

"The girls were both upstairs and either one of them could come down and out, if they were quiet," Lynn said.

"And Norma. Should we exonerate Norma? She was in the drawing room with us all evening, and came up to bed the same time we did."

Lynn pinched her lips together. "I don't think we can exonerate anyone at this point. Who knows what secrets Norma holds. She's a formidable actress, and could hide any motive. But I just don't see it."

"I don't see any of them doing it. We've got who was killed, and the how, but we need the why," Alfred said.

"Stop right there," Lynn said, and reminded him of Harriet's story of her accident and the botched surgery.

"Yes, that brings Harriet to the fore, doesn't it?" Alfred said. "Still, I don't think we should jump to an immediate conclusion. Any one of them could have gotten out of the house and back in the storm." He put his free hand behind his head and gazed at the ceiling.

"We need to sleep on it all, Alfred," Lynn said. "Right now, it's clear as mud. We're safe enough tonight, don't you think? If it was...her, then everyone else should be safe. Plus, no one else has any suspicions about murder, and we need to keep it that way for the time being. They think he fell in the empty pool and died."

"You're right, of course. If we don't get at least some rest, we will be useless tomorrow. We'll be fine overnight, considering everyone thinks it was an accident. Either that, or they're harboring notions about a random attack by someone from outside."

"Everyone but the real murderer thinks that." Lynn sighed. "I'm afraid a lot will be coming out in the morning."

"Which means," Alfred said, leaning to kiss the top of her head, "you need to sleep now. I'll stay up and listen for a while." Lynn opened her mouth to protest, but he shushed her with a finger on her lips. "No arguments. If all remains quiet, I'll probably drop off anyway. But first..." He got out of bed, dragged a chair to the door and propped it under the knob. "If someone tries to get in, we'll at least hear them coming, if they can get in at all." He crawled back in bed.

"Well, that does make me feel better. Thank you, Alfred." Lynn burrowed deeper under the blankets. He was right. They needed to be sharp in the morning, and he could fall asleep at the drop of a hat.

Just as she was falling asleep, she heard Alfred murmur, "It could be any of them. Or all of them."

~20~

In the middle of the night, Lynn awoke to find the spot next to her in bed empty. A wash of panic crashed over her. *Where is he? Alfred always sleeps as sound as the-* She stopped herself. Holding her distress at bay, she got up and, on the way downstairs, slipped on her dressing gown. She didn't even take time to slide into her mules.

No sound from the flirtation room, or any other room. She crept into the dining room. Empty. She went through to the kitchen. Sure enough, there he was, standing over the cutlery drawer. "Alfred," she whispered, hoping not to startle him, "what are you doing up at this hour? What are you doing, period?"

He swung around. "I didn't hear you come in, Lynnie. I hope you don't think something happened to me. I didn't want to disturb you." He turned back to the drawer.

Lynn joined him. "Knives. Is that what woke you up?"

"I haven't slept much, thinking about Tate. What was the weapon? What killed him," Alfred said. "To say nothing of who, who killed him."

Lynn went to him and leaned into his arm. "I know, darling. A very fitful sleep tonight, understandably. So, tell me, what have you found?"

"Look here," Alfred said. He gestured over the knife rack in the drawer. "All in place." He looked down at her. "Except one."

She waited with raised eyebrows. "And?"

"My meat cleaver. It's here." He showed her the cleaver, set up at an angle in the drawer next to the wooden knife rack. "It's not kept here, on the side. I always set it on top of the rack, like this." He demonstrated, picking up a dishtowel to handle the cleaver. He pulled it out and set it in its usual place. He frowned and shook his head. He picked up the cleaver again and brought it close to his face, turning it first to one side and then to the other. "Take a look, Lynnie. Take a close look. Tell me what you see."

She took a hold of his hand and bent to peer at the blade. "Nothing. I see nothing. Nice shiny metal. Clean, as usual." She let go of his hand and sent him a frown.

He turned the blade over. "Look at this side."

After grasping his hand again, she looked at the other side of the blade. Her frown deepened. "What's this?" She pointed, but did not touch, the blade where it joined the handle. She squinted and examined it closer. "Alfred, is that blood? That's blood!" She released his hand and looked up at him.

"Good. I was afraid I was seeing things." He looked around the kitchen. "I don't want to leave it where it was, in case... And I don't want to put it under our bed–"

"That's not funny," Lynn said. She crossed her arms and hugged herself. "I think you should put it back where you found it, just in case...someone...comes to check that it's still there."

Alfred stopped wrapping the cleaver in the dishtowel. "I'd rather hide it, maybe put it between two cake pans. Out of sight, out of mind. But I see your reasoning." He set the cleaver back on top of the knife rack and closed the drawer. He turned to Lynn and put his arms around her. "You know what this means, darling."

"We have a murderer in the house for sure." Lynn shivered.

"Let's get that chair back in place," Alfred said, shepherding them both back upstairs and into bed. He propped the chair under the doorknob and joined Lynn in bed.

"That's more than enough excitement for one night," she said, pulling the blanket up to her nose.

Lynn woke early after a short night of very little, and very fitful, sleep. She rolled over, groaned and opened her eyes to brilliant sunshine streaming in the bedroom windows. With an uncharacteristic quick movement, Lynn sat up. *No more snow! Marvelous!* She realized with a start that perhaps it wasn't so marvelous. They had a murderer in their house. And a dead body in their poolhouse.

Alfred, as usual, was already up. His side of the bed was unoccupied and cold. Undoubtedly, he would be in the kitchen, preparing breakfast. She remembered the cleaver. She swung her legs over the side of the bed and went into the bathroom. Time to get dressed and get moving. *I've got to talk with him this morning. We were simply too tired to do any more last night, and we couldn't actually do anything then anyway.* But now, now they must find answers.

The opportunity to talk vanished when she walked into the kitchen. Everyone but Norma was there.

Lynn headed for the telephone, with the hopes they could contact the police once everyone was in the dining room.

"Don't bother, darling," Alfred said, straining a cup of tea. "The phone service is still out."

"So I found out." Lynn stood with the dead receiver in her hand. She hung up the phone and sighed.

"Norma said she'd come down for breakfast," Lily said, apparently oblivious to the lack of contact with the outside world. "At least, that's what she said last night."

"Cup o' joe?" Ed asked Lynn.

She shook her head. "No, thank you. Tea for me, please."

Alfred was already handing her the cup he prepared. "Breakfast will be ready in a minute or two. I just put a ham in the oven, so we'll have something hot later." The fragrance of bacon was also filling the kitchen, even as he spoke. "The frittata is about ready to be served. I've kept it hot in the oven. Everything else is on the table."

He looked around at the group and smiled. "I had a lot of help this morning."

He's a consummate actor, Lynn thought. *I know he's rattled over Tate's murder and finding that cleaver.* She complemented Alfred's calm demeanor. "To the dining room everybody. First, grab a plate and have Alfred serve you here. I'll bring in the plate of toast."

They met Norma coming into the dining room. She was pale and a bit shaky, but dressed. "I...I'm hungry."

The rest swept into motion to bring food for her or pull out a chair. Nobody seemed to know what to say, so no one said anything, other than a soft murmur of sympathy.

Breakfast went off like synchronized swimming. Cutlery clinked on plates, the rush of juice poured into glasses, the slurp of coffee or tea, everything felt like it was choreographed to begin and end at the same time. That was foolish, of course, but the sideways glances and lack of conversation showed everyone attempting to reach the end of breakfast at exactly the same time.

When they lifted their napkins from their laps and settled them next to their plates, Lynn suppressed a nervous chuckle. Too well planned, it seemed. *It would never happen on stage,* she thought. *Too unnatural, too stiff. Unless to prove a point.* Nervousness at Tate's death, now that they had time to process the horror of losing someone. Lynn wondered if the rest knew about the amount of blood. Surely, if Ed noticed a lot of blood on his scarf, he would tell Harriet, and the information would flow from there throughout the entire group. Yet, because of the storm, maybe even Ed didn't connect with the amount of blood. Maybe there wasn't that much on the scarf. She couldn't remember. *Stop thinking about it!* she admonished herself. She realized everyone was finished eating.

"Let's help Alfred clear the table, and then move to the drawing room," she said, giving Alfred a rather pointed look. She got up and headed into the kitchen to deposit her dishes in the sink, where Alfred had prepared a soap-filled dishpan. The others followed her.

Lynn hung back as the group left the kitchen. "We have to work this out, Alfred. It's stopped snowing and the roads will be cleared tomorrow, or perhaps even later today. By then, we better know who...did this, or the killer will fly the coop." She took a hold of his arm and moved to whisper in his ear. "I think we should keep the cleaver between the two of us for a while."

Alfred nodded. "Agreed." They stood for a moment, sharing their unspoken concern. "Go with them to the drawing room. I need to check on something first. I have a hunch. It may be a while. Can you keep them occupied?"

Lynn knew better than to probe what he needed to check. Time was of the essence, and she trusted his judgment implicitly. "Of course, darling. Do what you need to do. We'll be fine."

She watched only as long as it took Alfred to go to the top of the back stairs and turn to throw her a kiss. She returned the kiss, and left the kitchen to join the others in the drawing room.

~21~

Lynn hurried to the drawing room. Her ears, attuned to the smallest noise in pursuit of Alfred's movements, heard the soft shush of the outside door being closed with care.

"Where's Alfred?" Harriet asked. "He doesn't need to do the dishes by himself." She turned to leave the room.

Lynn intercepted her. "No, he went downstairs to check the locks on the doors. And to see how deep the snow is in the courtyard, now that it stopped snowing. He'll be right with us." She slid her hand into Harriet's elbow and steered her toward the fireplace. "Help with the fire, will you?" She turned to Ed. "Can you re-light it? There are some paper scraps in the spill there."

"Not a problem. Used to be a Boy Scout." Ed squatted down on the hearth and laid out the logs.

Alfred's gone outside again, Lynn thought. *I heard the door close, but it looks like no one else did. What is he checking on now? Something else in the poolhouse?* She sighed. More waiting. She turned to the game table and gathered up the cards scattered across the surface. Leftovers from yesterday, before things got complicated.

No one seemed open to either conversation or work. They took up positions, as if in a scene on a stage, characters waiting for direction, perhaps from Alfred, once he returned.

Ed took up his usual post at the front window, keeping a close eye on the weather. Lynn could sympathize with his fidgeting foot, because she wanted the snowplow to make its appearance over the moraine as much as he did, apparently. Perhaps more.

Lynn pulled out the Scrabble game and dumped out the tiles. She gestured to Ellen and Lily. "Come on you two, let's see how many points we can pile up before Alfred gets back and we have to get to work. I'm a wicked Scrabble player. Think you can beat me?"

Ellen and Lily stepped to the table, and took up the challenge, chattering that they could give Lynn a run for her money. "Harriet can oversee and keep us honest," Lynn said. For a few minutes, only the click-clack of tiles being turned over and the crackle of the fire kept the silence at bay. Once the game started, the women were absorbed, or at least appeared to be, in counting up points. Harriet wrote everything down.

Halfway through the game, Lynn heard Alfred reenter the laundry room. His footsteps came up the stairs and continued through the flirtation room. The door to the drawing room opened, and Alfred stepped in. Lynn felt her heartrate return to something close to normal.

"It is bitter out there," Alfred said, affecting a shiver.

Lynn was sure it was affected. "Then let's get something warm into you. Come into the kitchen and help me make some cocoa or tea, or something." She turned to Harriet, who was hovering over the Scrabble game. "You're in charge, darling." She got up and ushered Harriet into her vacated seat. "Get some points for me." She took Alfred's arm and led him out.

Once in the kitchen, she swung on him. "I know you've got something, Alfred. Make some cocoa that we can take in, but talk to me while you're working. I'll get out the cocoa powder. And milk?"

Alfred nodded, then reached in his pocket and produced a pair of gloves. He set them on the counter and took over the job of cooking up hot chocolate. "I went to the poolhouse and brought these back."

Lynn picked up the leather gloves and examined them. "Are they Tate's?"

In the midst of pouring milk into a pan, Alfred shook his head. "Lynnie, my hunch was right."

"Alfred, stop beating around the bush!"

"When I went downstairs, I wanted to check on the coats. Remember Ed couldn't find his coat when he wanted to go back up to the cottage?"

"Yes, you both looked everywhere. No coat. What of it?"

Alfred pointed to the gloves. "Check the monogram on the cuff."

Lynn picked up one of the gloves and turned it in her hands. "E.W." She frowned. "Ed Wright? What was Tate doing wearing Ed's gloves?"

"He wasn't wearing them. I found them in one of the coat pockets." Alfred added the cocoa to the milk which began to steam. He kept stirring, but glanced at Lynn. "We couldn't find Ed's coat when Ed wanted to go up to the cottage because Tate was wearing it."

"What?" Lynn said. "How on earth? Why?" She stopped, hoping Alfred could fill in the blanks.

"Tate must have been in a hurry, didn't turn on the lights, grabbed a coat off the hanger."

"But Tate is so much taller than Ed."

"Indeed. That's why I went to the poolhouse just now. I had a suspicion. I think, in the back of my head, I noticed something odd about the coat Tate had on. Too short? Wrong color? I just couldn't put my finger on it."

"And?" Lynn patience was waning. She surmised what he was about to say, but didn't want to disturb his train of thought, or lead him off his own path. He needed to voice his own conclusion, not be swayed by anything she would say.

Alfred went on. "Tate had Ed's coat on. That's why he also had Ed's scarf. He didn't just somehow grab his own coat and Ed's scarf. He grabbed Ed's coat and scarf. When I checked, the coat on Tate's...body...was only down to his knees. And the sleeves were a bit short too."

"Didn't you notice when you moved his body into the poolhouse?" Lynn asked.

Alfred shook his head. He bent to check the cocoa, whose aroma was curling into the kitchen. "I had enough on my mind just finding...a dead body, without taking any details into account."

"And the gloves?" Lynn asked.

"In the pocket of the coat, as I said. That confirmed that the coat was Ed's, because his initials are stamped into the cuff of the leather."

"So, Tate was wearing Ed's coat and scarf," Lynn said.

Before Alfred could respond, Lynn heard the door from the dining room swing open. With frantic hands, she grabbed the gloves and shoved them in a drawer, barely getting the drawer shut as Harriet came around into their corner.

"Harriet!" Lynn said, then hoped she didn't sound too surprised. Harriet was the last person she wanted to see at this point.

"I just thought maybe you could use some help," Harriet said, her face puckering into a small frown. "Am I interrupting something?"

"No, no, not at all," Alfred said, his voice hearty. "Of course we can use some help. Lynnie, get down the pitcher for the hot chocolate, will you? Harriet, will you take a tray of mugs into the drawing room, please?" He flapped a hand at Lynn.

She got the message and pulled mugs from the cupboard before taking the pitcher to the sink. "Harriet, why don't you take the tray? I'll run some hot water in the pitcher, so the cocoa doesn't cool off so fast. Thank you." She sent a look to Alfred that said, *Don't leave the kitchen until we finish this conversation.*

Harriet picked up the tray while Lynn held the door open for her. The door swung shut behind her, and she was gone.

Lynn rushed to Alfred and hissed, "What next?"

"Now we tell them what I've found and watch their reactions," Alfred said. "That's about all we can do right now."

"We've got to get this sorted out before the plows can get out here," Lynn said. "I hope you know what you're doing." She dumped the hot water out of the pitcher.

"So do I!" Alfred answered, filling the pitcher Lynn handed him with cocoa.

Harriet's voice penetrated the door. "Are you two coming?"

"Yes, darling, on the way!" Lynn called.

There was no time for Lynn to voice what she was sure Alfred was also thinking.

~22~

Lily was perched on her favorite spot, the piano bench, as Lynn closed the door to the drawing room behind Alfred. Ed, Harriet, and Ellen were lined up on the settee opposite the fireplace, power in numbers. Norma sat slumped in one of the chairs in front of the fireplace.

Alfred set down the cocoa pitcher on the table by the piano, where Harriet deposited the tray with the mugs. He went to Norma and took her hands. "There is something you need to know, dear friend."

She looked him in the eye and nodded.

"We don't think Tate accidentally fell in the pool and struck the concrete steps."

Lynn knew he was trying to soften the blow by moving slowly, but she was nervous enough to mentally chew her nails. And she certainly didn't want him giving away that the two of them–as well as the murderer–knew how Tate was killed. They couldn't mention the cleaver. Not yet. That much was sure.

"Norma," Alfred said, "we think Tate was murdered."

The reaction was instantaneous. Gasps and "No!" all around.

Lynn was on high alert, trying to keep an eye on everyone at once. Harriet began to rise, but sank back and reached blindly for Ed's hand. Ellen pulled her feet up and set her forehead on her knees. Lily froze in place.

If they expected Norma to faint, or scream, or tear her hair, she did none of that. She let out a moan that was cut off with a deep intake of breath. Lynn saw her fingers whiten as she tightened her grip on Alfred's hands. But her gaze never left Alfred's.

They remained linked for several moments before Norma withdrew her hands to clasp them in her lap, and dropped her stare. Alfred moved to stand close by Lynn. The tension in the room didn't lessen by even a miniscule amount.

Then everyone started asking questions. "Murder?" "No!" "Why do you think *that?*" "Why?" The tone of it all was disbelief.

Everyone reacted but Norma, who sat catatonic.

Alfred held up a hand for silence, and the room became so quiet, they could hear the soft clink of a radiator. "Lynn and I have some things to share."

Lynn thought of the cleaver, still in the knife drawer. And Ed's gloves crushed into another drawer. She looked at Alfred and raised one eyebrow. He gave a quick sideways shake of his head. *No*, she read, *we agreed, not yet.*

"First, Tate was found in the pool, yes, but we don't think the fall killed him." He looked around at them all. "When I went back to check on...him, I wanted to see if there was anything that could tell us more. That, and to make sure he was properly covered and safe. I even went back to the poolhouse just now, to check again."

Lynn felt Alfred's tension. She wasn't sure how much he was going to reveal.

Alfred stood up. "Tate was wearing a camel hair coat. He must've picked up the first camel hair coat he touched. Which probably means he didn't turn on a light when he went down to the laundry room to get a coat and go out. That is what we thought from the start. He didn't turn on a light." He paced a bit.

Get on with it, Alfred, Lynn thought, trying to send out signals saying the same. But Alfred wasn't watching her.

"Remember Ed's white scarf was with his coat when he hung it up. And the scarf was found with Tate. Remember, when I came in, I gave it to Ed, and he showed it to us?"

"Yeah, it was really bloody," Ed said, earning an elbow in the ribs from Harriet. "Well. Gotta learn to keep my mouth shut, I guess." He got up and went to stand at a window. "At least it's stopped snowing."

"Alfred?" Lynn said.

"I didn't notice until I went back out this morning." He cleared his throat. "I wasn't paying much attention when I first found Tate, but then I realized...well, I wondered. So, I went down to the laundry room to check on everything this morning again. My coat is there. Tate's coat is there. But Ed's coat is not. Remember when Ed said he couldn't find his coat to go up to the cottage to go to bed? That's because Tate took Ed's coat. He grabbed Ed's coat-and his scarf-by mistake. I went to the poolhouse to see if my guess was right."

Lynn sat up, and picked up where Alfred left off. "You saw that the coat Tate had on was really quite short, almost up to his knees."

Alfred nodded. "Tate wasn't wearing his own coat. He was wearing Ed's coat and white scarf."

"So, in the dark, he took Ed's coat?" By Norma's widened eyes and parted lips, Lynn saw that Norma probably grasped the implication of it all. "Tate was the one who was killed. Why Tate? But a better question is, why not Ed? It was Ed's coat."

"Yes," Alfred said. "Tate went out, but he grabbed the wrong coat, Ed's coat and scarf."

"Which means ...." Norma looked up at Alfred. "Oh, no, Alfred. Tate had Ed's coat on. Was Ed the target then?"

"That's a distinct possibility," Alfred said. "Though perhaps someone saw Tate leave, knew it was Tate in Ed's coat, and went out after Tate with murder in mind for Tate, not Ed."

"But," Lynn said, "your first idea was that perhaps Tate was not—"

"Supposed to die!" Ellen's voice was a cry. She leaped up and went to kneel in front of Norma, covering Norma's hands with her own. Tears shone in her eyes. "Tate wasn't supposed to die," she whispered.

Norma blinked and looked directly at Ellen. "Of course he wasn't. He went out in that terrible storm and got turned around. How horrible to die by falling into the swimming pool! If only he stayed in the library, he'd still be here."

She refuses to really hear our suspicions of foul play, Lynn thought. *Understandable. Who would want to even entertain such a thought?*

Alfred turned toward Norma again, apparently to offer comfort, but Harriet stirred in her seat.

"Yes, he was. He was supposed to die." Harriet's voice was merely a murmur, but in the sudden quiet after Norma's words, everyone heard her. "Tate deserved to die."

Lynn restrained herself from showing any sign of emotion. She knew what was apparently coming. But she wasn't about to make a wrong guess. Let it play out. Perhaps she was wrong about any kind of revelation from Harriet.

Ed rushed from the window to go back to Harriet's side. He pulled her to him, holding her as she wept.

"He..."

"Shhh! You don't have to..." Ed said.

Harriet sat up straight. "Yes, yes, I do." She turned to them all and ran her finger down the long scar along the side of her face. "See this? This was done by *Doctor* Tate Alexander."

Norma seemed to return to herself. Her eyes widened and she leaned forward, ignoring Ellen. "Tate isn't a doctor. He's an accountant."

"He *was* a doctor when I knew him." Harriet and Norma locked eyes, so focused as to feel like they were the only ones in the room. "A plastic surgeon." Harriet took a deep breath. Norma waited. "You all know most of these scars are a result of a car accident. What you don't know is that Dr. Tate Alexander was supposed to fix all of this." She related the whole sordid story of Tate's drunken stupor and the slip of the scalpel, the severed nerve giving her a crooked face. "He did this to me. Made it so no one else could fix anything." She slumped into Ed. "He deserved to die."

Norma turned to Alfred. "You said you think Tate was murdered. Why did you say that? He fell into the pool. It wasn't murder." She seemed to be fixated on Tate alone, which was perfectly normal, considering the circumstances. Her comments did divert attention from Harriet, at least for the moment.

Alfred cleared his throat. "There was a lot of blood, Norma. We thought too much blood for just a fall and a crack on the head."

Lynn went to sit on a footstool next to Norma. "Remember the scarf. There was blood on the scarf. Too much, we think."

"Norma, Tate had a gash across his neck. He couldn't get that from a fall into the pool," Alfred said.

Lynn knew the blood on the cleaver would come up sooner or later. *But not now. Please, not now.* Alfred did not go on to mention the cleaver. Lynn breathed a bit easier. They still had something that only the killer would know.

"Murder," Norma whispered. "Is that possible? Murder?"

"If it's murder, then *you* killed him, Harriet!" Lily's voice cut through the room. Her tone softened as she added, "I can understand why, after what he did to you."

"No! I didn't kill him," Harriet protested. "But I can't say I'm sorry he's dead." Her forehead wrinkled as she pulled her eyebrows together. "Sorry, Norma." She slumped into Ed again. "But I didn't kill him."

"You certainly could have," Lily said. "You went up to the cottage to go to bed. None of us saw you after that. You could easily go out, and none of us would ever know. I'll bet he followed you up to the cottage. All you had to do was watch–"

"What would I be watching for?" Harriet said, confusion in her voice.

"For Tate," Ellen said. "Maybe you sent for him to come up to the cottage."

"Don't be ridiculous!" Harriet said. "Why would I want to meet with such a wicked man? The man who almost destroyed my life? Are you crazy? I'm sure he wouldn't want to see me any more than I'd want to meet with him. I was pretty sure he didn't even recognize me."

"Wait," Norma said. "Why would Tate follow Harriet if what Harriet says is true? That he damaged her." She sat up straight and put her hands to her cheeks. "If he did recognize Harriet, he never said a word to me. Going up to the cottage for any reason could be very dangerous for him." She swiveled to look directly at Harriet.

The phone in the kitchen rang.

-23-

They all twitched in their seats. Alfred went to the drawing room door. "The phone lines must be up. I'll get it."

"Darling," Lynn called, and Alfred turned. "It's probably Ben. Don't forget to ask…"

"Don't worry, I won't," Alfred said, heading for the kitchen.

I hope he got the message to have Ben call the police, Lynn thought. They were so attuned to each other, they often finished the other's sentence. She hoped this worked now.

No one moved around. No one talked. They fidgeted. But that was only to be expected.

Alfred was back. "That was Ben. He said the phone service is up and running. I know, pretty obvious." That brought a small ripple of relief. "He's calling the police." That slipped in without any fanfare. "The plows will be out working soon. But because we're not in an emergency situation, it will be a while before they get to us." He nodded at Lynn.

She tried to relax a bit.

Norma turned to them and spread out her hands. "What do you mean, Tate went to the cottage? He had no reason to go up to the cottage. Why would he go up there?" Clearly, no news about phones and snowplows was going to deter her from seeking answers.

"I think I can explain," Lynn said. "He *was* out in the storm. Tate *was* going up to the cottage." She went to Alfred, but he might as well have read her mind. He offered the note he found in Tate's pocket. Lynn took it and held it out so they all could see the name on the front. Harriet.

"Tate was bringing this note up to you, Harriet," Alfred said, turning to her.

Harriet sat up and disentangled herself from Ed's embrace. "Whatever for? He never came up to the cottage. I never saw him. Do you know what's going on, Alfred?"

"You better read the note," Alfred said.

"No," Harriet said. "I don't want to touch it. I have no idea what's going on. You read it out loud. Everyone might as well hear it." She sank back against the cushions.

Norma listened with her hands over her mouth.

"Are you sure?" Alfred asked. At Harriet's nod, he unfolded the note. "'Harriet. I'm writing this in case you won't see me.'" The silence hung heavy as Alfred continued reading. He ended with, "'I am truly sorry. Tate Alexander.'"

"What?" Ed's voice was thick with surprise. "He was coming up to *apologize*? Who was he kidding? I don't care if he gave up doctoring. What he did to you..." He reached for Harriet's hands and encased them in his.

Harriet sat stiff, with pinched lips, her hands encased in Ed's. Reactions like clouds scudded across her face. Pain, surprise, anger, collapse. "He was coming up to apologize."

Lynn nodded. "It appears so, Harriet. He was in such a hurry to get to you, he grabbed the wrong coat. I'm sure he didn't want anybody else to know he left to go up to the cottage. In his mind, perhaps this apology was something he felt was private, between the two of you. His mind was already on the way to you, so, without turning lights on, and distracted, he could easily take the wrong coat."

"So, consider the logic," Alfred said, "Would Harriet kill the man wearing that coat? Why should she? It was Ed's coat, so she'd see it as Ed coming up to the cottage, not Tate. She would recognize her own husband's coat, wouldn't she? That is, if she could see anything at all. It was dark and still snowing. Besides, she knew Tate was working in the library. She wouldn't expect Tate to come up to see her. Especially not in Ed's coat."

"Exactly right," Lynn said.

"Unless," Lily broke in, "Harriet told him to come up."

"I did no such thing!" Harriet was adamant. "No, I did not ask to see him. I *didn't* see him."

"If Harriet is telling the truth, that she didn't know Tate was coming, and didn't ask him to come up, then–"

"That means–" Ed said.

Norma broke in. "That means *you* killed him, Ed."

"What? What are you talking about? You crazy?" Ed's voice rose in volume. "Why would I do that? Because he took my coat? That's insane." By this time, Ed was standing.

"No." Norma's tone precluded anyone interrupting. "Your coat! Why would anyone care about your coat? You killed him to get revenge for Harriet's disfigurement." She seemed not to hear the gasps that ensued. "I'm sure she told you who Tate really was. If she couldn't do it herself–and I'm not leaving out that possibility–then you'd do it for her. Kill Tate, I mean."

Ed's face flushed radish-red and his lips tightened to a single line. His hands were clenched, and he looked ready to launch himself across the room. "I did not kill that man! I can see why someone would. Look what happened with my dear wife! Unforgivable!" Harriet reached out and pulled him back down next to her. "Well, you're right about one thing: I don't care that he took my coat."

"And there's the crux of the matter," Lynn said, projecting her voice enough so that no one would think to take the floor from her. Every face swung to her. "Ed's coat. Tate was wearing *Ed's* coat, not his own. Which means..." She gestured for Alfred to take over.

"Which means," Alfred finished, "*you* were the one meant to die, Ed. Not Tate at all. That was a fatal mistake."

Silence. Of course, Lynn was sure they weren't the only ones who realized this. But here it was, put out in front of everyone. Finally, perhaps they were all on the same page.

Ed put his hands on his knees and leaned forward. His face drained of color. "Me? What? Better yet, why?"

That got everyone else moving. Protests, murmurs of sympathy, head shakes, fluttering hands, and general incredulity. Even Norma sat up, rigid and frowning. Ellen went to one of the front windows and stood looking out. Lily joined her, shaking her head as she went. Ed stalked to the little game table across the room. Harriet walked with unsteady moves to the bottom of the stairs leading up to the library, where she dropped to one of the steps.

Lynn frowned. *There's no way to tell what they are all thinking with everyone scattered all over the room. We need to study faces, Alfred and I.* She glanced at Alfred and sent him a quick gesture that intimated the necessity of gathering them all closer soon. "We don't know why you were the target, Ed," Lynn said, "but we think it's pretty clear that it *was* you that was supposed to be the victim."

Lynn felt the tension and confusion in the room. Overwhelming.

"This is getting us nowhere," Alfred said. "We need time to think about all this. I think it's best we retire to the dining room. We can have some lunch and take a break. Maybe we'll come up with some better ideas."

"Thank you, darling," Lynn said. "That's wonderful idea. This is such a shock for all of us. Lunch will give us an intermission to organize our ideas." *And perhaps catch the murderer. Whoever it is might start to make mistakes. Between Alfred and me, we have the experience from the stage of paying attention to details that others miss.* She went to Norma and offered her hand. When Norma stood, Lynn looped her arm through Norma's and shepherded the group out of the drawing room.

~24~

Alfred placed a platter of hot ham, a cheese board, and a loaf of sliced bread on the table. Condiments and drinks were already set. "Don't start without me," he said. "There's a fruit bowl on the way."

Lynn opened her mouth to offer help, then thought better of it. They shouldn't leave the others alone, not even for a moment. She gritted her teeth, trying not to show her dread at being separated from Alfred, even for the short time it took for him to simply go into the kitchen and back.

He was back before her jaw began to hurt. She relaxed as best she could.

Considering how everything shifted into slow motion, it was clear no one was very interested in eating. At least at first, they simply went through the expected movements. Once they started eating, though, they seemed to realize just how famished they were. Ed, in particular, built a hearty sandwich. Lynn wondered if it was out of sheer nerves, or if he was simply reveling in still being alive.

Apparently, needless to say, no one was in the mood for conversation. They didn't talk about plays, or the jobs waiting back in New York, or even the weather. Nothing. Just the sound of knives scraping butter on bread, or slicing off a hunk of cheese. One would think they were at a dinner comprised of spies. *Well,* thought Lynn, *I suppose that's not so very far from the truth. We're all carrying secrets of one sort or another.*

Ed was working on a second cup of coffee, when he startled everybody by clearing his throat. "When do you think the roads'll be clear? When can we get out of here?"

That sent chills up Lynn's back, but she camouflaged her shiver by reaching for her teacup. They certainly couldn't leave soon. Not until they knew everything. Otherwise, they would scatter to the winds, assuming the trains were running, and the murderer would be gone in a puff of smoke. Would the police ever be able to prove who did it? It seemed unlikely, even if they were rescued by the snowplow. She shook her head.

By this time, Alfred was expounding on the unlikely scenario that had them all peacefully leaving anytime soon. "Ben said we'd be pretty much the last of the line, as far as the snowplow getting to us. We're relatively far out of town, and not on any main road at all. Nobody's getting out to work out here, I'm betting. So, we just need to sit tight and wait."

"So, we're supposed to sit around the table and grin at each other?" Ed's voice was indignant. "Sorry, Alfred, but it feels like we're in jail here."

Harriet waved a hand. "It's all right, Ed. The food is good, and the company is fi–" She broke off, her fidgeting showing how flustered she was. Clearly, the company was not fine.

"I wonder..." Ellen said, spearing a piece of fruit.

"What?" Harriet said. "What do you wonder?"

Ellen turned to her. "I wonder if someone came onto the estate and...um...killed Tate."

Lynn sent a pointed look toward Alfred. The cleaver. No one from the outside came into the locked house and found the cleaver to use. But she held her knowledge close, as did Alfred, even though the thought of a murderer sitting right there terrified her. At least, Alfred wasn't even looking at her, so the cleaver would remain their secret for the time being.

Norma shook her head. "No. I don't think anyone came from outside. Who knew Tate–and Ed, for that matter–was here? Nobody around here would have..." Her voice trailed off into tears.

"A beef with either of us," Ed finished for her. "Nobody outside of New York knows us. Well, at least, nobody knows Tate." He glanced at Norma. "Sorry, Norma."

"That's true enough, Ed," Norma said. "But someone might know you. You're a well-known playwright. And it *was* your coat, not Tate's."

Ed spread his hands and shook his head. "Unh. But why me? I haven't done anything. Have I?"

A chair scraped back from the table. "Excuse me," Ellen said, her voice shaking. By the time anyone registered her movements, and her reaction, she was up and out of the room.

"What's that all about?" Ed said. "Did I say something?"

Alfred stood up. "I should go with her. Maybe she feels sick."

Lynn knew exactly what he was thinking. *Don't let anyone out of our sight.* Lynn stood also. "I'll go, Alfred. If she's in the bathroom, she's not going to appreciate your attentions."

"You're right, Lynnie." He sat back down. "You'd better go check on her."

"I'll go with you." A surprise from Norma.

Lynn was grateful for Norma's offer. More than just for the company, Norma was the most logical to have along, seeing as how she was with Lynn and Alfred the whole evening of the murder, and the three went up to bed at the same time. Lynn nodded. "Let's check her room and the bathroom upstairs." They set off, leaving the doors to the dining room open, just in case someone–Ellen– appeared, or tried to steal past.

But Ellen was not on the bedroom level. The doors were open and no one was in any of the rooms, including the bathroom. When they returned downstairs, Lynn heard a door slam below, as if it came from the laundry room. Norma grasped Lynn's arm, and they paused a moment to listen for more noise. There was nothing. The rest of the party watched from the dining room, but no one moved.

"What's Ellen doing down there?" Norma whispered.

Lynn shook her head. "Trying to leave, maybe? But Alfred locked all the outside doors last night, and took the keys with him. She can't get out. Come on."

"I think she's terrified for some reason," Norma said as they started down the front main staircase.

Lynn didn't want to entertain thoughts of why Ellen panicked.

At the bottom of the stairs, they swung around to enter the laundry room, but the door was shut tight. "This is what we heard, I'll bet," Norma whispered, close to Lynn's ear. "The laundry room door being closed."

Lynn, with infinite care, turned the knob and slid the door open. They slipped in. But the room was empty, the coats and boots still hanging. Hanging, but swaying a bit. Ellen must have tried to get her coat, before she realized the outside door was locked. Lynn gestured to the back stairs leading up to the kitchen. She sent Norma up to check if Ellen went that way, while she waited at the bottom. That was unlikely, as any one of them in the dining room would hear her.

Norma was back in a moment. "No, no one in the kitchen. Where could she be?"

"Well, she's not here." Lynn sighed. "Let's go back into the foyer. She's got to be down here somewhere."

The door to a small room off the foyer was wide open, and it was clear no one was there. Norma walked to the front door, peered outside, and turned to whisper, "There are no footprints in the snow out there, so she's not outside." She rattled the doorknob. "Besides, the door is locked."

Lynn crooked a finger at Norma and went to a door behind her. "Closet," Lynn whispered.

The two women positioned themselves in front of the closet door, just in case Ellen would burst out. Though where she would go

was uncertain. There was nowhere to go with them blocking the doorway.

Lynn poised herself to be ready for the rush of a body, and swung the door open.

In the corner, curled into herself, sat Ellen. Ellen looked up, tears running down her face. She wiped her nose on her sleeve and looked up at them.

She looks like a waif from Oliver Twist, Lynn thought. She reached out her hand. "Come. It's time to rejoin the others." What else was there to say? They knew nothing more, but Ellen's bolting was certainly a reason for concern. Lynn knew they needed to get Ellen back upstairs before they said another word.

"I–" Ellen began.

But Lynn cut her off with a firm shake of her head. "Don't say anything. We need to be together. Come on." She beckoned, inviting Ellen to take hold and get up.

Ellen nodded, wiped her nose once more, and reached out to take Lynn's hand.

Lynn saw how unsteady Ellen was, and put her arm across Ellen's shoulder as she led the girl up the main staircase, and back into the dining room.

-25-

Lynn escorted Ellen to her chair, then joined Norma in returning to their seats also. "She was hiding in the foyer closet. Scared, indeed."

"What the hell, Ellen?" Ed, of course. "You can't just go running off like that."

Harriet set a hand on his arm. "Give her a chance to catch her breath, darling. This whole...situation is very stressful. Take some time to–"

"Wait," Ellen said. Everyone swiveled to fix on her as she turned to them. "I need to tell you. I..." She gulped and turned back to Norma. "I pushed him. I pushed him into the pool. I knew Ed went out to go back to the cottage. I knew he would leave the house here when he was finished in the kitchen with the rewrites he was working on. I–" Ellen crunched her fists tight and drove them into her eyes. "I killed the wrong man!"

As she began to cry, the others were shocked into silence.

"I have to tell you this before I lose my nerve." Ellen took a deep breath. "I saw a man leave and I followed... I thought it was Ed. Before I went out, I thought I heard him on the stairs. His coat wasn't in the laundry room either. And...and...once outside, I thought I recognized his coat." She pulled a handkerchief out of a pocket and swabbed at her eyes.

In the sudden silence, it felt as if everyone stopped breathing. "Go on, dear," Lynn encouraged.

Ellen nodded and spoke without looking up. "The snowstorm was terrible, and I didn't know if I'd be able to see him out there. But I did see someone leave the courtyard before I lost track. When I got closer to the cottage, I spotted him. He was stumbling close to the pool. He must've gotten off course in the storm. So, I...I came up behind him and...and...and pushed him in. I heard a crack as he hit...something. Maybe a stair, maybe the bottom of the pool." She shook her head. "I ran. I came back to the house and went to bed." Her voice broke. "I couldn't really run, the snow was so deep, but I got away as fast as I could." She turned to Norma. "I couldn't believe what I did. Even then, I couldn't believe it."

Norma's face was drooped and pale, but she held her rigid posture, and was silent.

Lynn went to Ellen and set a hand on her hair. "Why kill Ed in the first place? It doesn't make sense."

Ellen looked up, balled her fists again and beat on her knees. "My sister. He killed my sister!"

Ed stood up and backed away from them all. "What the hell? I never killed anybody in my life! What is she talking about?"

"You killed her!" Ellen was suddenly animated. She rose, tipping over her chair, and rushed out of the dining room.

Everyone swept out right behind her. They followed her to the drawing room, where they found her sitting upright on the floor, her hands splayed next to her.

She started rocking back and forth. "I have to tell you. I know I have to tell you." She whispered, "I don't want to." She looked up at them all clustered at a distance from her. "But I have to, don't I?" Before anyone had time to react, she picked up the thread of her tale again. She turned to point at Ed. "My sister committed suicide after you showed her as evil, a drug addict, a...a...whore!"

"What?" Ed's face was twisted with fury. "What are you talking about!" He opened his hands and held them palms up, as if pushing her words away.

Lynn said, "Slow down, Ellen. Tell us what you mean."

Ellen closed her eyes and took a deep breath. Eyes still closed, she said, "Ed Wright wrote a play about a woman who was a slut, a drug addict, a thoroughly evil woman who caused the death–the suicide–of her lover, another woman." She opened her eyes and drilled a look at Ed. "That play killed my sister. You wrote that play, knowing exactly what you were doing. *You* killed my sister." She closed her eyes again. "I admit it. I wanted to kill you. I tried..." She buried her face in her hands. "I killed the wrong man."

"You didn't kill the wrong man," Harriet said from her spot on the settee. "You killed the wrong *person.*"

Ed rushed to his wife and sat down next to her. "No, darling, please. We've talked about this. Now isn't the time."

"Yes, Ed. Yes, it is. Now is the best time, the only time." Harriet took his hands and turned to him. "We wanted to do this sooner or later. Maybe this forces it out." She turned to the others. "You see, *I'm* the writer. I'm the one who writes the plays. I'm the culpable one." She shrank down in her seat. "So, you see, Ellen, you didn't kill the wrong man. You killed the wrong person. I'm responsible."

"No, she's not, Ellen. My ideas go into our plays too," Ed said. "This time, this play, it was my input. Harriet had no idea who that character was based on, if anyone."

Lynn said, "Ed, please explain. I am in the dark here, and I think the rest of us are too."

Ed went on. "I did suggest the character. I did base it on an actress out of control that I knew in the past. I knew...I didn't think anyone would recognize who it was based on, and it was a perfect fit for what we wanted." He cleared his throat. "I didn't tell Harriet any of this."

"Lynn and I know most of the plays, but I don't recall this one," Alfred said. "What play are you talking about?"

"It was way off Broadway," Ed said. "The title was *She Knows Too Much.*"

Ellen's crying turned to gasps and gulps. She gained control of herself, leaned toward Ed and hissed, "He used my sister's nickname. I knew right away what he was doing, slandering my sister." She struggled to her feet and moved as if to face down Ed.

Alfred reached out and led her to a chair, where she sat, upright and stiff. Everyone but Ed shrank back and chose seats.

"Wait." Ed held up a hand to stop her. "How do you know it was about your sister?"

"I was in New York a while. After my sister ran away, she sent me one postcard, and it came from New York City. No return address. Just a line that she was okay and working. She was an actress, like we both were in Chicago. After my mother died, I brought that postcard to New York, hoping for a miracle, hoping I could find my sister. I had a good acting reputation, and some recommendations, so I could find work. I figured if I went backstage at enough plays, I'd run across someone who would remember my sister. Finally, at *She Knows Too Much*, I did. A member of the cast told me all about 'Mimi'." She made air quotes around the name.

"I knew of Mimi," Norma said. "I heard she committed suicide. But the main character in Ed's play wasn't named Mimi. She was called Millie."

"No, you're right. The character's name wasn't Mimi," Ellen said. "But he found out her childhood nickname: Millie. Her real name is Amelia, but I couldn't say Amelia when I was little. So, I called her Millie." She dissolved into tears again.

"So, your sister Amelia was also known as Millie," Lynn said. "But when she got to New York, she took on the stage name, Mimi?"

Ellen nodded. "Everyone knew her as Mimi. They didn't know her as Millie. But someone did. Ed did. I recognized the Millie character in the play as my sister."

Lily stood up from the piano bench. "I knew her." A mere whisper of sound.

Lynn felt the tension and the confusion in the room. Overwhelming. She herself felt at sea. They all needed a moment. Probably several, in order to sort this out.

-26-

Ellen put her handkerchief to her lips. She swiveled to Lily. "You knew her? Millie, I mean."

Lily nodded. "She wasn't Millie when I knew her. She was already Mimi. I'm so sorry, Ellen. She was...a grand person."

"Mimi," Ellen whispered. She pushed her hands tight against the floor. She looked around the room. "When she left Chicago, she was a mess. She was almost everything that Millie was in that play. A drunk, a drug addict, a sex fiend. She used people and threw them away. But never, never did I see her cause anyone's death." She set her elbows on her knees and bent to clasp her hands in front of her mouth. "We tried everything. Mother even threatened to send her away to an institution. That's when she ran away. We never heard a word, until I got that postcard."

"So, you went to New York to try and find her," Norma said.

"She was my sister," Ellen said, rising and slumping into a nearby chair. "I had to try. She was so miserable. I just wanted to help her."

"I don't think she was everything that the character Millie was, dear," Harriet said.

"Yes, yes she was," Lily whispered. "Someone she knew did commit suicide. Because of her." She put her hands over her face. "Please..."

"How? How do you know her?" Ellen's whisper matched Lily's.

"We…we…," Lily said.

"C'mon, Lily," Ed said. "Come clean. You two lived together. Everybody knew that."

Lily pushed herself upright, setting the piano bench rocking in the process. "What do you know, Ed Wright? Ellen's right! You killed her. You killed her as sure as if you fit the noose around her neck yourself!" She grabbed hanks of her hair in her hands and wailed. "You did the right thing, Ellen! You did!"

Alfred steadied the piano bench, then stopped at a look from Lynn. No one else moved.

"How did you know Amelia…Mimi?" Ellen looked up at Lily, her face the picture of pain.

"We…worked together a few times. And, yes, we shared an apartment," Lily said. "She found some things hard, even in New York."

Ellen nodded. "Chicago was hard on her, too…hateful for her. She had to get out. No one who knew us, even the theater people, could accept that she was…what she was. She lashed out by soaking herself in things that would make her forget."

Lily took up the tale. "So, she came to New York to shed all that. I'm here to tell you that she did. It took her a while, but she did." Lily swiped at a tear. "She found herself. She found me. I was her best friend." She shot Ed a look of pure vitriol. "Until your play. You destroyed her. Maybe Harriet's right, maybe Harriet knew none of this. Then it is all your fault, Ed. Too bad Ellen killed the wrong person."

Ellen shook her head. "I'm so sorry…"

Lynn and Alfred shared a glance, and Alfred left the room. Within moments, he was back, carrying the cleaver wrapped in the dishtowel. "I'm sorry, Norma, to have to do this." He unwrapped the cleaver to show them all. "Tate was killed by a blow to the neck with this." Without fanfare, he rewrapped the weapon. "There's a touch of blood where the blade meets the handle."

"Alfred is a fanatic about his kitchen tools, so we know it was clean before…" Lynn stopped. "The police will surely confirm that the blood is Tate's."

"This means," Alfred said, "if Ellen only pushed him into the pool, she did not kill Tate." He gestured to Ellen. "Come here, Ellen. I want to show you all something."

Ellen's eyes grew large, and she started to shake.

"Don't worry, dear," Lynn said. "He has no intention of using that cleaver on anyone. Alfred, put the cleaver on the sideboard, please." She turned back to Ellen. "Go on over. Trust me."

Ellen sidled to where Alfred waited. The cleaver sat on the sideboard, far from anyone. "Look. Ellen is short enough to fit under my arm," Alfred said, turning his back to her. "Ellen, reach over my shoulder, will you, please?"

She couldn't stretch quite that far.

Alfred turned around to face everyone. "Ellen couldn't have killed Tate. Tate is as tall as I am, and she wouldn't be able to reach up that far, much less deliver a fatal blow to the neck. She doesn't have the reach or the strength." He gestured for her to sit down in a nearby chair.

"So, if Ellen didn't do it, who did?" Ed asked. "She had the motive."

"A most pointed question," Alfred said.

"Look at the facts. Let's go through this," Lynn said. "Norma was with Alfred and me in the drawing room that night, rehearsing and drinking. We three went up to bed together."

"And Norma would have no reason to kill her own husband," Alfred added.

"But it was supposed to be *me* who would be killed," Ed said. "Tate had on my coat and scarf. Someone mistook him for me."

"Yes, but Norma has no reason to kill you either, Ed," Lynn countered. "I think that's clear."

"Well, *I* certainly have no reason to kill Tate," Ed said. "Wearing my coat isn't any kind of reason."

"No, but you wanted revenge on Tate–Doctor Tate–for what he did to Harriet." Lily's voice pointed out the obvious.

"*No!* I tell you no! I did not kill Tate." Ed's voice was furious. "I was working in the kitchen. I didn't even know he was out there!"

Lynn went to him and led him to sit beside Harriet on the settee. "We're simply looking at all the angles, Ed. All of them. Any possibility."

"Doesn't help," Ed grumbled. "But I didn't kill him." He slid back and folded his arms across his chest, as if in defiance. "I didn't."

<h1 style="text-align:center">-27-</h1>

"So," Lynn said, taking charge, "one possible suspect: Ed." She held up a hand to stop Ed from interrupting. "Let's just leave it at that and examine any other possibility."

"If Ed didn't commit murder, that leaves Harriet and Ellen and Lily as possible suspects to consider," Alfred said. "Agreed?"

Lily said. "But Ellen already said she killed him."

Lynn shook her head. "No, she said she pushed the man she thought was Ed into the pool. But Tate didn't die from a fall."

"He died from the slash to the throat," Alfred said. "Even if Ellen was convinced she killed Ed, she really didn't. And she didn't kill Tate either, as you saw with my little demonstration. She couldn't reach that far."

"Then Harriet did kill Tate!" Lily said. "Look what he did to her face. She had every reason in the world to kill him."

"Why would I kill my own husband?" Harriet asked. "Because Tate had *Ed*'s coat on. If I got that close, I would recognize the coat and scarf, wouldn't I? I would assume it was Ed." Her voice rose in indignation. "Besides, I was asleep in the cottage and had no idea what was going on outside."

"Right, Harriet," Alfred said. "In addition, Ed was your partner, and your shield from the outside world. The world who couldn't accept a...damaged woman playwright."

"There are women playwrights," Harriet said. "People like Lillian Hellman. But none look like me. I was a nonentity, a pariah. Without Ed, no one would mount my work."

"You give me too much credit, my dear," Ed said.

"Time for that later," Lynn said. "Harriet is in the clear."

"But how on earth could someone get out of the house, kill Tate, and get back without being seen?" Norma asked. "And how did *Tate* get outside?"

"We know he went out to deliver the note of apology to Harriet in the cottage," Lynn said. "We know he grabbed Ed's coat by mistake, probably in the dark, because he didn't want anyone knowing he was going out. All of that is easy enough. He was in the library, so he could easily go into the little hall where the bathroom is. From there, he could slip through the flirtation room and down the main staircase, get a coat from the laundry room, and leave the house. The sound of the wind that night would obscure most other sounds, and the snowstorm would make it hard to see very far, or very clearly."

"Whoever went out could follow the same way, assuming they saw him leaving, and thought it was really Ed," Alfred said. "Ellen or Lily. Which one of you? Now, we really need to examine which one of you."

"I told you," Ellen said. "I pushed him. I went upstairs early, because I knew Ed would have to go up to the cottage sometime. I sat at my window and watched. I could see the outside door to the main house here from my room, and I could see just enough between wind and snow to see him leave. I did see him leave. At least, I thought it was Ed. So, I bundled up and sneaked downstairs, just as Mr. Lunt said. I had to force my way through the snowdrifts. By the time I caught up with him, he was veering away from the cottage. I...I saw him stumble to the edge of the pool. He didn't hear me coming. I didn't see anyone else. I...pushed hard on his back, and he fell into the pool." She put her hands to her face and shivered.

"The key word there, my dear," Lynn said, "is 'stumble.'"

"Someone already slashed his neck before you pushed him," Alfred said. "He was dying. You pushed him, but you certainly didn't kill him. That means–"

"Lily." Norma stood up, her hands curled into fists. "That means Lily killed my husband."

Heads swiveled to fix on Lily.

"That's not possible," Lily said, her voice unwavering. "If Ellen left when she saw Ed...Tate, then how could I, or anyone, get there ahead of her?"

"Ellen probably saw you, Lily," Lynn said, "when she saw a figure in the snow from her window. You yourself must've seen someone step outside before you went up, and assumed it was Ed, considering you recognized Ed's coat, and maybe his scarf. As for Ellen, it would take her a while to get dressed to go out, and then to get downstairs without being seen. But you could make a quick exit. Once outside, and the deed done, the lawn is long enough, and you could hide alongside the poolhouse if you saw Ellen coming. Easy enough to hurry back to the house without anyone being the wiser."

"But I went up to take a bath, remember? I was cold," Lily said.

Ellen frowned. "I heard her in the bath when I got back to the house. When I went down the hall to my room, I heard the water running."

"The bathroom adjoins Lily's bedroom, with a private door between," Alfred said. "The bedroom and bathroom doors lock, so she could have left the water running slowly, or gotten back early enough to turn on the water. She would've been back in the house before you, Ellen, at any rate, even if it was only by moments. Enough time for her to dash upstairs and lock both bedroom and bathroom doors, and turn on the tap."

"And rinse the cleaver in the tub. She could return the cleaver to the kitchen later, when everyone was fast asleep. Is that how it went?" Lynn waited for a response. "Lily?"

Silence deepened to a point of oppression.

"Just because I'm tall? Is that why you think I killed Tate?" Lily's voice was indignant, but her eyes looked both angry and terrified.

"Something else is going on here," Lynn said. "Lily, you knew Ellen's sister. You even said you shared an apartment. You knew her well then."

Lily nodded. "Yes, she was my best friend. But I didn't know she was Ellen's sister. I only found out the same time you did."

Lynn looked askance at Lily. "Your best friend. Was she, perhaps more than just a best friend?" It was a gentle probe, but one designed to confirm Lynn's suspicions.

A deep pause heavy with questions waited for Lily's response. It took a long time coming. But when it did...

"She. Was. My. Lover!" Lily's voice was loud and hard enough to make everyone jump. Tears streamed down her face. "Mimi was my lover, my heart, my soul. Yes, we were lovers." She dropped onto the piano bench. "Ed destroyed her. Mimi knew the character of Millie in the play was based on her. She couldn't live with that old life surfacing. The woman who committed suicide on her account. And all the rest." Lily gulped, though tears continued coursing. "Mimi hanged herself! I tried to get past that horrible night, but I couldn't. When the opportunity came to work with the Lunts in one of *his* plays..." She hissed and turned to face Ed.

"You thought you could finally avenge Mimi," Norma whispered.

"Yes," Lily said. "Yes. But I killed the wrong man." She spun on the bench and dropped her head onto her arms on the keyboard, creating a dissonant cacophony. "I never meant..." Her weeping almost drowned out her words. "I'm sorry, so sorry...."

The grumbling sound of a snowplow approached and turned up the drive, putting everyone on alert.

-28-

In the late afternoon sunlight, the county sheriff and his deputy rolled into the courtyard right behind the snowplow. The plow rumbled its way around the courtyard and out again, leaving the sheriff room to pull up close to the house.

Lynn waited in the kitchen with the two girls, while Alfred went down to meet the officers. Ellen, tears in her eyes, sat at the kitchen table, clenching and unclenching her hands, and looking only at the floor. Lily stood silent, ramrod straight, looking defiant.

Lynn heard Alfred and two men coming up the stairs.

"-to the poolhouse to take some photos of the crime scene," Dan, the sheriff, was saying as Alfred ushered two men into the kitchen. Lynn knew them both.

"Thanks for coming right away, Dan," Lynn said. "It's a terrible situation."

"Easy enough to follow the plow. At least the wind's died down mostly. Too bad we had to come out for such a reason." Taking off his gloves and hat and laying his coat across a kitchen chair, he indicated Lily and Ellen. "These the perpetrators?"

Alfred nodded. Dan's deputy strode to the girls and restrained them both with handcuffs.

"Okay if we use your dining room?" Dan asked. "We need to get statements before we take them in to the county jail."

"Wait!" Ellen cried. "What about my things? I don't have anything down here. Can't I go get my things? Please?"

"Where–" The sheriff was interrupted by Lynn's hand on his sleeve.

"It's all right, Dan. We'll gather their things. Unless you need anything else from us right now?" Lynn said.

Dan shook his head. "Not at the moment. Mr. Lunt filled us in with the basics downstairs. We'll get to you in a bit."

Lynn nodded, slipped her hand through Alfred's elbow and said, "Come, darling. Let's get out of their way."

The third floor was fairly quiet when they reached the girls' room at the top of the main stairs. The door to Ed and Harriet's room was slightly ajar, and Lynn could hear them moving about and talking, but couldn't make out what they were saying. No reason to disturb them. Hopefully, they were packing. No one wanted to stay around, which was fine with Lynn.

Norma's door at the end of the hall was closed and not a sound could be heard.

They slipped into the girls' room and located the suitcases. Alfred said, "Where they're going, they're not going to need any of this. Don't spend time folding. Just fill the cases up."

Lynn didn't take time to look at each individual piece, simply crumpled garments as she stowed them. It was easy enough to tell tall Lily's clothes from short Ellen's, though it probably didn't really make a difference as to what went into each suitcase. But her sense of order had her sorting anyway.

Making the rounds of the room to check if they forgot anything, they made quick work, and were soon headed back to the kitchen with the two cases. The men and girls were gone from the kitchen. Lynn could hear them on the stairs, so she and Alfred followed them down, where the two girls were already dressed in their winter coats and boots.

"You two are real troopers," Dan said to Lynn and Alfred, as they emerged in the laundry room. "Thanks for holding 'em until I could get here." He turned to his deputy. "Put those two in the car. I left the engine running. Stay with 'em."

The deputy hustled Lily and Ellen to the door and opened it, allowing a blast of cold air into the room. "Let's go." He grabbed their suitcases.

Ellen turned to Alfred, "What's going to happen to me, Mr. Lunt?" Her face was full of dread.

"Get yourself a good lawyer, Ellen," Alfred answered.

Lily said nothing.

The girls were escorted out to the sheriff's car and handed into the back seat.

Alfred closed the house door and turned to Lynn. "A sad situation, Lynnie. They both had such bright futures."

"Give me a minute," Dan said. "I got most of it from Alfred, but let's hear it again, now that you're both here."

Lynn and Alfred related the whole story, filling in details for each other as they went.

Dan asked a question now and again, nodded in understanding, shook his head when the details of the murder were told, and finally, when the account was finished, sighed. "A shame, a real shame. But all the stories jive, so far."

Lynn cocked her ear. "I hear another car." She went to the door and peered outside.

"Yeah," the sheriff said, "I called Walter. That's probably him now."

A hearse plunged up the drive and beached itself in the courtyard like a shiny whale, the black crisp against the white snow.

Alfred joined her at the door. "Yes, it's Walter and Mary from the funeral home."

"I want to go up to the poolhouse myself," Dan said. "Mr. Lunt, you think you can help us?"

Lynn said, "You go ahead, Alfred. I'll just go upstairs and…I don't know…keep Norma company, I guess. I think Ed and Harriet are still packing. I hope we can get Norma off before they come down." Lynn set her finger on her lips and frowned. "I'll just make sure Norma will have privacy." With that, she hurried up the steps to the kitchen.

When she reached the kitchen, she saw Norma seated at the small table. *What can I possibly say?* she thought.

As if reading Lynn's mind, Norma said, "I know you don't know what to say, Lynn. But there isn't really anything one can say at a time like this, is there?" She swiped a handkerchief across her nose. "It's just so...horrible."

Lynn pulled up a chair and sat down, reaching out to take Norma's hands. "Alfred is..." What to say? Just say it and be gentle. "Alfred is helping the mortician and his wife. They'll get Tate tucked away safely, and take you to the train depot."

Norma nodded, her lips pressed tightly together. She closed her eyes and inhaled deeply. "Just let me know when they're ready. I have our valises here ready to go."

"Let me check if they're ready for you." Lynn picked up one of the suitcases and hurried down the steps to look outside.

Alfred, the sheriff, and the undertaker were already next to the poolhouse, having followed a ragged trail forged through the snowbanks. Walter, trailed by Alfred, carried a rolled canvas stretcher. They disappeared inside, and before long, they were back, bearing Tate's body, out of sight in a black bodybag. The men took the body to the hearse and slid it in the back.

Lynn opened the door for the three men. They turned to go upstairs, but Dan asked Walter to remain in the laundry room. "I need to take statements from the others," he said. "I'd like to talk with the widow first, if that's okay?"

"She's in the kitchen," Lynn said. "We can go up and tell Harriet and Ed you'll be with them shortly. Is that workable? They're still in the bedroom, packing."

With Dan's nod, they went all the way upstairs, leaving him with Norma in the kitchen.

Lynn took Harriet into another bedroom, while Alfred stayed with Ed. Before long, Dan came upstairs and thanked them for separating the couple. "Better this way. Shouldn't take long. The stories are all the same," he said.

Lynn was able to return to comfort Norma in the kitchen while Alfred stayed upstairs.

Norma was at the kitchen table, sitting next to Mary, the undertaker's wife, when Lynn came back. "Ed's coat," she said. "How can–"

Lynn sat down on her other side and patted her arm, silently knowing Ed couldn't get the coat back, now that it was part of the murder investigation. "Ed already said to keep it with Tate." A little white lie, but a humane one.

Norma gulped, closed her eyes and nodded.

When Alfred came back to the kitchen, he went straight to Norma and took her hand. "You'll be free to go in a minute."

"We'll take the train to Milwaukee," Norma said.

"The roads are cleared," Mary broke in. "We'll take you in to Milwaukee. Walter can help you make any arrangements you need to make. No arguments about that now. It's the least we can do."

Norma's shoulder dropped a bit, and she sighed. "Thank you. I'll stay in Milwaukee until I can...have Tate cremated. Then, we'll go back to New York together." She looked out at the sunlight pouring through the trees. "I'm going to retire. We were talking about it anyway, and we can afford it. Tate always wanted to go someplace warm, someplace like Santa Fe. He kept talking about the art scene in Santa Fe. That's where we'll go. I'll sell the apartment and probably be gone by the time you two get back to the city. So, this is truly goodbye."

Lynn hated to say anything about the coat situation, but she gulped and forged ahead. "Tate's coat–"

Norma waved a hand and cut her off. "I can't...You just take care of it." She covered her face with her hands, took a deep breath and said, "Give it to someone. Give it to…Ed…anyone. It will remind me too much of–"

"We'll take care of it, Norma. Not to worry." Alfred reached out to touch her shoulder in sympathy.

Dan came back into the kitchen. "You can go," he said to Norma. Don't worry about anything. We're all set here." He turned to the Lunts. "I'll take the girls in and get the paperwork finished. If we need you, I'll call. But I think we can close this out quickly, thanks to you two."

Norma stood up and stretched to kiss Alfred's cheek, then turned to do the same for Lynn. Mary approached, linked her arm with Norma's and led her downstairs. The Lunts followed. Norma turned just before going out, deep grief on her face. A small moment, and she was gone.

"Oh, Alfred, I don't know if I can do this anymore," Lynn said, closing the outside door.

Alfred put his arm around Lynn and turned her toward the stairs. "Let's go back up. I'll call Ben. He can come and drive Harriet and Ed to the train station."

Once upstairs, Alfred picked up the telephone and was giving the operator Ben's number when Ed and Harriet came into the kitchen.

Ed was carrying all of their luggage. "I'll take these down."

Lynn was caught between aversion and sympathy. After all, it was Ed's play, more than Harriet's, that began the juggernaut that ended in a murder at Ten Chimneys. Yet, and yet… How horrible he must feel when an innocent man became his inadvertent stand-in. Yes, Tate caused Harriet's disfigurement. The old Tate, not the reformed Tate they knew. Did he deserve to be murdered, especially at this distance of time? Perhaps. She was not the one to judge.

Then there was Harriet. Lynn felt the strongest for her. She remained blameless, somewhat of a pawn in Ed's hands. And Tate's too, if it came to that.

A rush of pity and compassion washed over Lynn. That's what their guests all deserved, even Lily and Ellen. Pity, mostly, for the two girls, but still, mixed with compassion. All those threads weaving together over the years, culminating in horrible karma.

Lynn was jolted out of her reverie as Ed came back up the stairs.

Alfred handed off Ed's gloves, retrieved from the kitchen drawer. "We thought these might tell us something, Ed, but they really didn't add anything. I took them from your coat pocket when I went up to the poolhouse to examine Tate one last time."

Ed took the offered gloves with a nod and slapped them on his palm. He frowned, then lifted his head and looked from Alfred to Lynn. "I...I am truly sorry to bring...all this...down on your heads. I was so blind."

Harriet slid her arm through his. "Perhaps we can work..."

Alfred set his hands on the back of a kitchen chair. "Perhaps. We're open to examining any scripts."

"I understand," Ed said. "If anything good comes out of this, it's that from now on, our billing will be 'Written by Harriet Stevens and Ed Wright.'" He turned to Harriet and planted a kiss on her cheek. "I was so wrong not to include her. Wrong and stupid."

"You're doing it now, though, Ed," Lynn said, her voice quiet. She could feel how hard it must be for Ed to make such a significant change.

"Don't worry, I'll keep him in line." Harriet's attempt at levity fell somewhat flat, but Lynn felt the truth of what she said.

"I think I hear Ben's car." Alfred turned to Harriet and Ed. "He'll take you to the depot. There are late trains from Milwaukee that will get you back to New York overnight. He'll make sure you catch the train from here in to Milwaukee."

The four of them made their way downstairs. Alfred helped Harriet into her coat while Ed put on his galoshes.

"Um, Norma said to offer you Tate's coat," Lynn said. "Your coat...well..."

"I don't want any coat," Ed said. "It's better my coat stays with ...well, with..."

"Take Tate's coat," Lynn repeated. "It's still winter out there."

"I can't bear to look at Tate's coat, Lynn," Ed said. "I'll just tough it out. I'll be on the train soon anyway."

"It's far too cold out for that." Alfred reached for an old coat he used on cold days doing farm work. "Here, this'll suffice. You can always drop it at the Guild theater in New York. It'll find its way home from there."

"I really don't think–" Ed began, before he was cut off by Alfred.

"No, go ahead, take it." He handed off the coat and went to the door. "Ben's here already."

Ben came into the laundry room, picked up the luggage and retreated to the car.

Ed put on Alfred's coat and pulled it tight against his chest. He shook out the arms, showing sleeves that needed to be turned up to accommodate his shorter arms. "I'll get it back to you." He cleared his throat. "I don't think a thank you is really sufficient. I hope I can make it up to you both somehow." He looked down, as if he couldn't bear to look at them.

Harriet slid her arm through his, and they set off for the car.

Ben drove down the driveway, and was gone in moments.

They were all gone, back–or forward–to wherever their lives would take them.

•　　•　　•

Once coats and galoshes were stowed, Lynn and Alfred went up the back stairs and through the kitchen. Alfred cleared the dining room of detritus and dishes, and Lynn found a radio station that filled the kitchen with soft songs. They worked without conversation, lost in their own thoughts, right through washing the dishes and putting the leftovers away.

The radio shifted to George and Ira Gershwin's "Our Love Is Here to Stay" just as the last of the soapy water gurgled down the drain. Alfred was drying his hands when Lynn came up behind him and put her arms around his chest. "Let the rest of the dishes air dry, darling. Come dance with me. I need your arms around me. I need to feel safe."

He turned and drew her in. She rose on tiptoes, set her cheek on his and closed her eyes. The radio sang into the kitchen.

Alfred swayed to the music and hugged her closer. "They'll be all right."

Lynn whispered in his ear, "I know. We will too, darling." She could feel his warmth seep in, filling up her heart.

AUTHOR'S NOTE

Deserving of Murder is fiction hanging on a framework of fact. However, I created enough that it's better to call the whole thing fiction, rather than trying to explain what is, and what is not, real. That being said...

Lynn Fontanne and Alfred Lunt were indeed real-life premier stage actors from 1919 to 1960, and did own Ten Chimneys, an estate in rural Wisconsin, to which they retreated every summer. The house is filled with plenty of nooks and crannies, stairways and hallways. Though there's never been a murder there, it would be a perfect place for one!

Lucky for us, Ten Chimneys, house and estate, is open to the public, May into December. Check out the Ten Chimneys website: http://www.tenchimneys.org for more information and photos.

ABOUT THE AUTHOR

After earning Bachelor and Master degrees, Mary Ann Noe spent 29 years in Waukesha classrooms, first teaching 7th grade Language Arts and Social Studies followed by 22 years of high school English and Psychology. Upon retirement, she joined a writing workshop where she reinvented herself as an author.

Mary Ann published, through Black Rose Writing, the novels *To Know Her*, *A Handful of Pearls*, *Hannah's Eyes*, and *Water the Color of Slate*. Her non-fiction essays and poetry are in numerous print and online magazines. She spends time reading, writing, baking, and happily communing with nature in Wisconsin. Visit www.maryannnoe.com for her blog, a collection of photos, a contact link, and more.

OTHER TITLES BY MARY ANN NOE

NOTE FROM MARY ANN NOE

Word-of-mouth is crucial for any author to succeed. If you enjoyed *Deserving of Murder*, please leave a review online—anywhere you are able. Even if it's just a sentence or two. It would make all the difference and would be very much appreciated.

Thanks!
Mary Ann Noe